SURVIVAL!

HURRICANE

OPEN SEAS, 1844

K. DUEY AND K. A. BALE

ALADDIN PAPERBACKS

FOR THE WOMEN WHO TAUGHT US THE MEANING OF COURAGE:

ERMA L. KOSANOVICH
KATHERINE B. BALE
MARY E. PEERY

———————

First Aladdin Paperbacks edition March 1999

Aladdin Paperbacks
An imprint of Simon & Schuster
Children's Publishing Division
1230 Avenue of the Americas
New York, NY 10020

Book design by Steven M. Scott
The text for this book was set in Bembo.
Printed and bound in the United States of America
10 9 8 7 6 5 4 3 2 1

Library of Congress Cataloging-in-Publication Data
Duey, Kathleen.
Hurricane : open seas, 1844 / by K. Duey and K.A. Bale.
—1st Aladdin Paperbacks ed.
p.   cm. — (Survival! ; 9)
Summary: During almost four years at sea with her whaling captain father,
thirteen-year-old Rebecca finds life both boring and difficult—especially when
the ship is nearly sunk by a hurricane.
ISBN 0-689-82544-7 (pbk.)
[1. Whaling—Fiction. 2. Hurricanes—Fiction. 3. Sea stories.]
I. Bale, Karen A. II. Title. III. Series: Duey, Kathleen.
Survival! ; 9.
PZ7.D8694Hu   1999
[Fic]—dc21   98-50386
CIP   AC

CHAPTER ONE

The rising sun was still half hidden by the sea, and the sky was dark blue overhead. Rebecca peeked around the corner of the deckhouse, toward the stern of the ship. Papa was at the helm, his calloused hands steady on the dark, worn wood. Mr. Adams was standing beside him. They were both scanning the calm surface of the ocean.

Rebecca turned and peered toward the bow. She had to find Major. None of the men would appreciate having her cat underfoot while they worked. If Mr. Nilsen saw Major wandering the deck, meowing, he might do something awful to him.

Peeking around the deckhouse again, Rebecca saw that her father was still preoccupied. Not that it mattered. It had been nearly two years since he had stopped chalking the line on the deck, but she knew precisely where it had been—and she was still forbidden to cross it for any reason.

"Rebecca? What are you doing?"

Her brother's sudden whisper made her turn. Joseph was ten—three whole years younger than she was—but he often got to go anywhere he wanted on the ship. Sometimes, Rebecca hated him for it. Then she would feel guilty and sinful.

"Rebecca?" Joseph insisted.

"I can't find Major," she whispered back.

Joseph wrinkled his brow. "Mama said to tell you to come back down."

Rebecca pulled in a long breath of the fresh sea air and let her gaze drift out over endless gray water. Sometimes the ship seemed as tiny as a piece of straw floating in a puddle—and she felt trapped upon it, like an ant that could only pace back and forth. "At least ants don't have to worry about which end of the straw they should keep to," she said aloud.

"What are you talking about?" Joseph demanded.

She shook her head. "Nothing. Tell Mama I will come down as soon as I find Major."

"I'll ask Papa if I can go forward and look for him. But he's probably just up in the pantry looking for rats."

Rebecca shook her head. "No, I saw him come abovedecks."

"Then I'll find him."

Rebecca smiled gratefully. "Will you?"

Joseph nodded, and she could see his eyes twinkling. Any excuse to leave the deckhouse was welcomed on these long, tedious days. They had had fine weather lately, but they hadn't spotted a whale in over a month. Papa had finally set a ten-dollar bounty to keep the men sharp.

Rebecca knew that her father was determined to return to New Bedford with a thousand barrels of oil. Mr. Tildon was an exacting shipowner who demanded the best from his captains—or they were asked to seek work elsewhere. A full hold would also mean that Papa wouldn't have to go right back out awhaling.

Joseph was passing the mizzenmast, stepping around a circle of men who sat hunched over, splicing rope. Three or four more of the foremast hands spoke in low voices, leaning against the rail, staring out at the smooth water that lay calmly all the way to the horizon.

Rebecca glanced back along the wall of the deckhouse. Papa was still talking to Mr. Adams. So long as she stayed where she was, he wouldn't notice her. Rebecca turned toward the bow again.

Mr. Jackson, the oldest hand onboard, was seated near the main mast, his back against the brick wall of the tryworks. He was carving steadily on a big sea lion tusk. He was always scrimshawing, etching intricate designs into whales' teeth or sea lion tusks—whatever kind of bone was at hand. At least he had something real to show for all his idle hours, Mama said. His wife sold the decorated ivory to an English merchant.

Mr. Adams's voice, coming from the stern, startled Rebecca. He was striding forward, snapping out orders to the men leaning on the rail. They moved slowly toward the main hatch, surly expressions on their faces. Joseph turned and watched them pass, and Rebecca knew what he was thinking.

At dinner the night before, Papa had warned Joseph to stay out from underfoot. There had been a fistfight. Papa had put both the men in irons for a few hours, then let them go once they had calmed down. Mama was worried. She said all the men were irritable, and some of them were dangerous.

Everyone had gotten uneasy and impatient during the past weeks. The grease and blood from the last whale had long been scrubbed out of the decks, the ropes were all in good repair, and the sails had been mended. There really was little to do now, but wait—and everyone was sick of that.

Rebecca spotted John Lowe, still up in the rigging. He had been up in the crow's nest every chance he had gotten for the past three days, and Rebecca knew why. The ten-dollar bounty would mean more to the young freed-man than it would to almost anyone else onboard. He was working off a debt his father owed Mr. Tildon. Rebecca liked John Lowe. He was quiet and polite and he was always kind to Major.

"I found your stupid cat," Joseph sang out as he came around the copper water tank by the mizzenmast. Rebecca grimaced, furious with him for giving her away.

"Rebecca Anne?" Papa called out. "Are you there?"

She stepped forward, keeping her head slightly lowered so that Papa wouldn't think she was being impudent. "Major got away from me again," she said, just loudly enough for him to hear. She glanced up through her lashes. Joseph was walking toward her, the black-and-white cat relaxed and comfortable in his arms. Rebecca reached out. Major accepted the transfer calmly. He yawned, rubbing his whiskers against her neck.

Just then, Mr. Adams came striding back across the deck. Rebecca was glad for the distraction. Joseph edged forward, and Rebecca knew that he was trying to overhear whatever

Papa was saying. In spite of his terrible seasickness, Joseph wanted to be a whaling master when he was a man.

Using the moment when no one's eyes were upon her, Rebecca slipped along the far side of the deckhouse. She went down the narrow stairway and pushed on the door with her shoulder, turning sideways as she emerged into her father's chart room.

Major struggled, and she held him closer. "You have to stop running abovedecks like that," she whispered fiercely. "If something happened to you, I don't know what I'd do." She laid her cheek on his soft, warm fur, then let him down, reaching back to close the door tightly.

"Rebecca?"

"Yes, Mama?"

Rebecca heard the sound of scissors. Her mother was cutting cloth for a new shirt for Joseph. It would be Rebecca's turn next. She looked down at her sleeve, ending a handspan above her wrist now.

"Did you find Major?" Mama called.

At the sound of his name, the big black-and-white cat rubbed against the side of the horse-hair sofa, arching his back and meowing.

Rebecca heard her mother laugh from the next room. "I have my answer, I suppose," she called out. "Unless you have taken up yowling like a cat."

Rebecca half-smiled at her mother's joke, wishing, as she so often did lately, that some miracle could bring her friend Hope and her cousin Elizabeth to her for a day's teasing and fun.

Trying to control the lonely tears that stung her eyes, Rebecca looked around the captain's room. Papa's charts were in here, and Mama's best trunks. There was a good glass oil lamp on the little table beneath the shelves that held the few books her parents had brought with them.

Major stretched up, digging his claws into the rug. It was Mama's pride, a dark green Brussels carpet with a pattern of tiny red flowers woven in.

"Stop him, Rebecca," Mama's voice came through the open door.

Rebecca scooped Major off the floor and shook her finger in his face. "You know better than that," she whispered, scolding him. She reached out to close their stateroom door. Papa didn't like Major's silky black fur on his bedlinens.

"Will you come give me a hand?" Mama called.

Rebecca took two quick steps across the narrow room and looked in the doorway that led to the forward cabin. All the mates' stateroom doors were closed. They were either asleep or up on deck. The skylight was wide open today. Mama said her eyes were getting bad. It was becoming difficult for her to sew by lantern light.

"Come hold the cloth in place, will you please? It will save me having to baste it."

Rebecca let Major jump to the floor. She positioned herself near the end of the long Scotchman's table, close to the thick mizzenmast that rose through the polished surface. Mama used the table for laying out pattern pieces. It was awkward unless she removed the low partitions that ran along the edges, but that was so much trouble that she usually didn't. The rails made using the table for anything but meals difficult, but without them, supper plates would slide onto the floor when the seas were high.

Leaning across the rails, Rebecca spread her fingers wide on the blue cambric as her mother began to cut.

"How much longer do you think we will be at sea?" Rebecca asked, without glancing up at her mother.

"I have told you—"

"I know, but does Papa say anything about it?"

"It depends on the last whale or two, Rebecca. Your father won't allow a return until—"

"Do you think it will be before Christmas-tide?"

Rebecca watched her mother's face go stiff and stern. Home wasn't a subject Mama liked to dwell upon. Sometimes, it seemed like a vague, half-remembered dream-place to Rebecca. She could barely picture the shell-paved streets and the grass and trees at the edge of town.

She could recall Elizabeth's quick smile and Hope's long dark hair very clearly. She could imagine them standing on the dock and she would never forget how she had felt when Elizabeth had thrust the cloth-covered box into her hands—and she had heard the mewling of a kitten. It had been almost four years since she had seen Elizabeth and Hope. Major had grown into a lanky tomcat—a living link to her two best and most precious friends.

"Rebecca? Pay attention, please."

Rebecca let the cloth go as Mama reversed it, then continued cutting. The deck rose gently beneath her feet, then fell. Maybe the flat calm would end today. Rebecca sighed. She wanted to ask her mother again how long it would be before they got home, but she held her tongue. She never got an answer, and it just irritated Mama's already short temper. She could only hope and pray that it would be before her fourteenth birthday. She did so want to celebrate it with her friends.

Rebecca's first birthday aboard the *Vigilance* had come when they were less than three months out of New Bedford, coming down the coast toward the horn. Her second had come on a day so stormy that she had spent it cowering and nauseated in her bed, unable to stop imagining the clifflike gray waves that rose beneath the *Vigilance*, then dropped away again.

The third birthday had been the best, except that Papa had been gone, leaving her, Mama, and Joseph in Lahaina on the island of Maui. There were missionary families living there, and other Christian wives waiting for their husbands to come back from hunting right whales in northern seas. Lorrin Andrews, the seaman chaplin, and two girls had played hostess for a real party. Rebecca wondered if she would ever see either of them again.

"Put that daydreaming mind of yours to some use," Mama said, interrupting her thoughts. "Read or add a round or two to your knitting."

Rebecca sighed and thought about Joseph,

walking freely up on deck. She envied him fiercely.

"Rebecca? I'm finished."

Rebecca lifted her hands, hoping that Mama wouldn't give her the usual lecture about not paying enough attention. The ship's clock began to strike six.

"I am going to make biscuits later today," Mama said. "You can help with that."

Rebecca nodded dismally. Biscuits for the thirty-odd men aboard took hours to make. But it kept the cook and the steward happy when Mama helped out. Some ships' ladies were demanding and bad-tempered. Mama was convinced that she could conquer any man with kindness and patience—and up to now, it had worked. Before yesterday's fistfight, Papa had only had to punish three of the men so far—and very lightly. Hanging them up by their thumbs for an hour had brought them around. None of the officers had ever been insubordinate.

It was unusual to have such a peaceable voyage. Everyone said so. Papa was a fine shipmaster, and Mama was the kind of woman who made petticoat whalers better to work on than those without captains' wives aboard.

"Read a little, Rebecca," Mama repeated as she picked up the shirtfront and her thimble. "Get busy at something and you will feel more settled."

Rebecca went and pulled her knitting basket out of the corner and sat on the sofa. Major curled up beside her. She stared at the yarn and the ivory needles Mama had let her use, but she could not force herself to take even a single stitch.

CHAPTER TWO

From the platform up in the crow's nest, John Lowe heard Mr. Adams call the change of watch. The men were already coming up out of the forecastle. They were not usually this eager to begin a day's work. John knew it was the bounty.

John hesitated. If he climbed down now, Mr. Adams would send someone else up the rigging—there would be no shortage of volunteers this day. It wasn't fair. First watch had a much better chance of sighting a whale in the daytime than second watch would ever have at night.

John ran a hand across his eyes and scanned the water. There were no ripples, no distant plumes from spouting whales—nothing. He squinted, trying to ease his aching eyes. He had been on duty all night. He was always tired at the end of his watch, but this morning his eyes were exhausted from staring into the darkness for twelve hours.

"All below that wants to eat!"

It was Mr. Hawkins, the short-tempered cook. His shout brought the idlers off the rail, and John sighed. They had been on short rations for weeks, and missing a meal was unthinkable. His belly ground painfully with hunger almost constantly, and he knew that ignoring it would only make him weak and dizzy later on. He would have to go belowdecks with the rest of the second watch.

"Move yourselves!" Mr. Hawkins shouted again, then he turned and went back down through the main hatch.

From his perch in the rigging, John watched as men started toward the forward hatch. He forced himself to stay put, scanning the water with careful intensity, hoping for a stroke of good fortune. Sometimes sunrise brought whales up to sound. John turned very slowly, covering the water's surface in quadrants, the way he had been taught. When he had gone around the full circle of the horizons, he sighed again. Then he straightened the ends of the cloth he had wound around his head to keep his too-long hair and sweat from blinding him.

Russell had given him a worn-out shirt to tear into strips, and John was grateful. He had lost his cap overboard in a high wind rounding the horn. A new one from the slop chest would cost more than he wanted to pay. He started down the rigging.

When John's boots hit the deck, he walked stiff-kneed for a few steps, his legs cramped from the long night. The first watch was still coming up from belowdecks in twos and threes while the last few from John's watch headed down.

"What are they cooking up?" Mr. Garner groused as he fell in beside John. "Rancid pork? Or do we have more hard worm-bread this morning?"

"Isn't it biscuit day?" John asked, and looked up to see Mr. Garner's watery blue eyes brighten.

"Is it? But even so, that won't be until supper."

"Biscuit day?" Mr. Jackson said from just behind them.

John turned to look into the older man's grim face. He was too old for this kind of work. Most of his teeth were gone, and he was thinner than anyone else. John watched him fumble with his long-stemmed pipe.

"Got a match, boy?"

John nodded, reluctantly pulling out the little waxed box he always carried. The pipe smokers used up their matches and went bumming for more.

"I think the lady will be baking for us today," John said carefully as he handed over a single match. "I'm not sure of it."

Mr. Jackson nodded brusquely to show that he had heard and wouldn't hold John responsible if there weren't biscuits later on. But there was a wistfulness in his eyes that was unmistakable, and John knew exactly what he was feeling. The hard, rotting bread that they ate with almost every meal got worse with each day that passed. Biscuits, fresh and hot, the flour weevils barely visible, reminded everyone that they were human beings, civilized. And most of all, having something to look forward to would make this day different from the one before and the one that would follow.

"'Morning, John," Russell Greene sang out. "The bunk is ready for you, lad."

John nodded at the older man. Even now, when the food was wormy and short, Russell always had a tale or two about worse times. He claimed to have been on a whaler once that had hit such rough weather, the berths had never dried out—not once in two years. On that same voyage, he said that half the crew had been tied up for lashing to keep them aboard in port.

The captain's name had been Hannover. If Russell was telling the truth, Captain Hannover had even sealed up one mutinous crewman in an oil cask. He had hauled the poor fellow all the way back to New Bedford in the ship's hold, barely feeding him enough to keep him alive, crouched in his own filth.

"You'd better get down to the galley, right quick," Russell whispered as John passed him.

"There's rice, but not much of it, I think. Plenty of hardtack and molasses."

John nodded, grateful for the warning. He hurried to get ahead of the ten or twelve men who were still lingering abovedecks, hoping that the first daylight would bring them a sighting—and the ten-dollar bounty. John hesitated once more, turning a full circle, scanning the surface of the water before he whirled and ducked down the stairs and into the companionway.

After a night abovedecks, the heavy stench of the forecastle hit him hard. John passed by the tiers of bunks, casting a glance at the one he shared with Russell. As usual, the dirty bedclothes were tangled. Russell slept like a dog, turning and burrowing himself deeper into the blankets. Sometimes the rope-webbing that formed the bottom of the berth was pushed awry, and John had to straighten the cords or risk slipping through.

John waited his chance to get past the Salazar brothers. They had just awakened and stood side by side, bare-chested, laughing over some private joke. These two sea-toughened Portuguese men had always scared John. He tried to stay out of their way.

Turning sideways, John slipped around the foremast and opened his trunk. His tin plate and spoon were on top, and he pulled them out, then shoved his water cup in his jacket pocket. He wrinkled his nose. He was used to the sour, sweaty smell of the forecastle, but it still bothered him sometimes at mealtime. One or two of the men used soap to wash on Sundays, but most of them didn't bother. The bedclothes had been aired a few weeks before, but it had done little good.

John walked through the narrow area between the berths that lined the walls, then followed a ragged line of men through the cooper's workshop and the nearly empty storeroom. Almost no one was talking this morning. The night had been long and dull enough that most had had to fight to keep awake. John felt the heavy weariness that came with boredom.

The galley was crowded. Most of the second watch and some from the first were waiting for the cook to fill their plates. When his turn came, John held out his tin and fidgeted as Mr. Hawkins ladled a dollop of wet rice next to a piece of hardtack. Then he laid down the ladle long enough to spoon molasses into a dark, lumpy puddle next to the bread. Without a word, he turned to the next man.

John filled his cup with brackish water from the oak barrel that stood in the corner. Balancing his plate and walking slowly, he went back up. No one was eating in the forecastle today, he noticed as he walked through and glanced in at the empty berths. Usually by now, the second shift was bedding down, their plates licked clean and repacked in their trunks.

On the deck, John leaned against the rail, taking small bites of his rice to stretch the meal. He knew that the brownish specks were bee-tles, killed by the boiling, but he no longer thought about it much. He dipped his hardtack in the molasses and savored the pungent sweet-ness, ignoring the gritty pieces of dirt. He pushed aside only the recognizable fragments of the cockroaches that had invaded the molasses casks. The hardtack made his teeth ache, as always, but he gnawed at it hungrily, his eyes moving constantly across the water.

A wind was picking up, and the surface of the sea was ruffled. The first watch was hauling up the sails. Captain Whittier was pacing the bow, waiting for his first mate to complete the shouted orders. John glanced around the deck.

Almost everyone had come back up, and they were all gazing out to sea. Aft, by the deckhouse, John could see Joseph Whittier, the captain's son. He was a merry little boy, and most of the crew liked him. There was a daughter, too, a meek girl named Rebecca, but of course she was kept as far as possible from the men.

John wiped up the last of molasses with his fingers and sucked them clean. Then he lowered a bucket to fetch up seawater to rinse his plate. No one taunted him about it anymore, but two or three of the men still smiled when they noticed him washing his spoon and cup.

John stood at the top of the stairs, reluctant to go below. He had to be the one to see the next whale. He had to be. Captain Whittier was not likely to ever offer another bounty, or at least not on this voyage—and John was hoping never to come on another. His mother had wept for three days before he had shipped out, but it hadn't made any difference to his pa. John was through hating his blacksmith father for striking the bargain with Mr. Tildon that traded four years of his life for a new English forge. But he still hated whaling.

John took one last look at the ocean, then turned and bolted back down the steep stairs. The men from his watch who were too tired or too discouraged to stand abovedecks watching for whales were scattered around the forecastle, talking in low voices.

Boston George winked at John from his berth. "You're going to break a leg, coming down them stairs that fast."

"Don't you worry about me." John smiled at him, and George laughed.

"I forget, you're just a young pup. Wait till you're twenty-five like me. Then you'll see how bad a pair of knees can ache."

John glanced toward the companionway.

Usually, he liked talking to George and Russell before he fell into his berth to sleep. But today was different. He wasn't going to sleep at all—not until he had spotted the whale.

"Aw, go on, then," George said, gesturing broadly. "I know what you're up to. A man as shortsighted as I am would be fool to give up any sleep over a bounty."

"Sleep well, George," John said, lifting the lid of his trunk and sliding his cutlery inside. Then he turned and headed back abovedecks.

"Please," Rebecca said for the tenth time. She could tell that Mama was about to give in or get angry, and Rebecca was willing to take the risk. "Joseph has been out all morning, and you haven't worried about whether or not he is too chilled," she added in a wheedling voice.

Mama looked up from her sewing. "I told you to read, or add to your bedcover."

"I'm so tired of reading and knitting, Mama." Rebecca tried to sound persuasive, but found herself fighting tears.

Mama looked up again. "Patience is the soul

of a woman's virtue, Rebecca. You had best learn that."

Rebecca stared down at her feet, biting her lip. Her mother was right, and she knew it, but there were times when she could barely stand their little rooms. More than anything, she was sick of the endless ocean that trapped them upon the ship.

Mama stood suddenly and laid down her scissors. "All right, then. We shall go out into the air for a bit. Do us both good."

Rebecca leaped to her feet and followed her mother back through the after-cabin, stepping around the enormous sofa and the end of her father's massive chart table. She scooped Major up from his favorite chair and carried him against her chest up the steep stairs that led abovedecks.

Out in the open air, Rebecca pulled in a deep breath, turning to take in the expanse of sky, still rosy with sunrise in the east. The sails were up now, and she gazed at the fluttering canvas. There wasn't much wind, but the awful calm had lifted. Rebecca saw that Mr. Adams was at the wheel now. Papa was up close to the bow, talking to the men.

Major wriggled in Rebecca's arms, and she set him down. He instantly ran forward and she chased him, picking him up again.

"Oh, let him go, Rebecca," Mama said. "No one will hurt him, and he catches a rat now and then, Mr. Pratt says."

Rebecca heard the tightening in her mother's voice as she spoke the steward's name. They got along on most counts, but lately Mr. Pratt had been questioning some of the foodstuffs Mama requested.

"Joseph says a rat can kill a cat if it's big enough."

"Your brother is only trying to tease you," Mama said with a laugh. "A cat is too smart to chase a rat that big."

Rebecca held on to Major, half-turning to avoid her mother's disapproving eyes.

"Your father only agreed to let you keep that cat if he was a hunter. You baby him and feed him too much for him to earn his way."

Rebecca didn't answer, but she set Major

down and let him move toward the main hatch. If one of the crew decided that Major wasn't worth the scraps of meat and bread he ate, he might just disappear, and she would never know what happened to him. Papa said a ship was the most unforgiving place on Earth, and Rebecca thought he was right. She shivered, remembering the two men Papa had had to punish.

"Whale! There she blows! She blows!"

Rebecca felt a chill. She recognized the voice and spotted John Lowe, leaning out over the rail, pointing, then turning back to shout again. A second later, the cry was picked up by three or four more men.

Rebecca saw her father stop midstep and whirl around to stare out to sea. Then he raised his hands to his mouth and shouted, "Lower away!"

The deck became a scramble of activity and confusion. Then, as Rebecca watched, the motion began to sort itself out. Boat steerers ran to the lockers to get their harpoons and irons. Men began to unwrap the ropes that held the boats solidly in their davits along the ship's rail.

Mr. Adams shouted orders beside his boat. Mr. Salazar's men were all experienced, and he rarely bothered to shout anything at all; they knew their jobs. Mr. Stevenson, the second mate who usually headed the third boat, stood by, waiting.

Rebecca watched intently to see what her father would do. She heard her mother's sharp intake of breath when he dismissed Mr. Stevenson. Papa was going out with the others.

CHAPTER THREE

John's elation over spotting the whale was soon lost in the melee. He had been an oarsman for nearly six months, but every time he sat in the whaleboat, he still fought a terror so deep, it seemed to grip his very bones. He had told Boston George about it once and had been glad to hear the older man say that he felt it, too.

Ducking beneath the mainsail and dodging around the winches that lined the starboard side of the deck, men scrambled into the boats. The coils of rope shrank as the davit lines were passed through the wooden pulleys. Mr. Garner sat facing the stern, somber and staring. John positioned himself between Mr. Forbes and Mr. Jackson, his hands lightly on the butts of his oars as the winches creaked and squealed.

As the boat settled in the water, John looked astern. All four boats were in the water now. The Salazar brothers had not taken time to button their shirts. Antonio was the best harpooner aboard, and Francisco was boat header—the only one who wasn't an officer. He had been whaling so long that even Captain Whittier had to admit he was more qualified than Mr. Potter, the fourth mate.

John turned to look at Boston George. He was standing tensely in the bow, his eyes moving across the water, his jaw set so hard that the cords in his neck stood out. He gripped his harpoons in one hand, the coiled whale lines hanging over his shoulder.

"Break out the oars forward," Mr. Adams shouted.

John lifted his oars almost in unison with Garner, Forbes, and Jackson. He could see Mr. Garner's oars trembling and knew his own were unsteady. This was the hardest part, before anything happened, when nerves and tempers ran high.

"All ready?" Mr. Adams was stern-faced and pale.

From the bow, John could hear Boston George beginning his prayers, chanting the words. He would go on chanting, John knew, until the whale was floating dead in the water.

"To my count," Mr. Adams roared. Then he began the cadence, and John lowered his oars, putting his back into it. The boat moved across the water. At the top of his next stroke, John looked over his shoulder. They were headed almost straight into the sunrise.

When he could, John craned his neck, glancing behind himself, trying to see what he had seen from the deck—the forward-arching spout of a sperm whale. The hard pulling steadied him, calming him. The cadence was quick, but even Jackson kept time without lagging.

"There she is, boys!" Mr. Adams shouted. "Port side."

John turned his head without breaking rhythm. In the distance, a whale breeched, its squared head breaking the surface. A milky spume came from its blowhole.

"To my count," Mr. Adams shouted again, and the cadence changed, speeding up. He dipped his long steering oar into the water and leaned against it, turning the boat slightly. They skimmed across the water now. The Salazars were close, matching their speed. The other two boats were farther back, though not much behind.

"She blows, hard starboard!" Mr. Adams shouted.

The cry made every man turn to see two more plumes shooting skyward. The two slower boats veered off, the boat headers shouting back and forth to make sure neither whale was lost. The Salazars' oarsmen kept up a killing pace and drew even with Mr. Adams's boat. John bent his back, sinking his oars deep and bracing against the pull with his legs. He heard Boston George's prayers speed up. Behind him, Mr. Jackson was breathing hard, but John knew he wouldn't quit. He never did.

They kept up the rhythm until Mr. Adams shouted for them to rest oars. The Salazars had angled off to the south, John realized suddenly.

They must have seen a fourth whale. John twisted around and caught a glimpse of one of the other boats, lying almost directly beneath the arched curve of a whale's flukes. He could see the early sunlight glittering through seawater that exploded upward as the whale's tail sank, slapping the surface.

"She blows!"

Mr. Adams's voice brought John around just as the boat lifted and fell, jolting so hard that John dropped his right oar. He heard Boston George curse, then begin to pray again as the boat was slewed sideways by a sudden, rising ridge of water that appeared without warning. John could see roiling currents tangling and colliding beneath the surface.

Was the whale directly beneath them and coming up? John fumbled for his oar, gripping the wood. He had heard stories of sperm whales attacking whalers' boats, breaking them into splinters with their huge, stubbed teeth. The boat rose again, and this time, John saw something moving close to the boat, three or four feet beneath them.

"Stern! All oars!" Mr. Adams yelled.

John reversed his stroke, watching Mr. Garner's and Mr. Forbes's oars flash in the sunlight, trying to stay in unison with them. The boat caught and hesitated, then moved backward. John imagined the whale beneath them and felt a cold sheen of sweat on his brow and the back of his neck.

"Rest oars!"

John lifted his oars out of the water and sat still, breathing hard. Mr. Adams was leaning out over the stern, peering at the water. "Hold her steady," he shouted without looking up.

"At the ready, sir," Boston George called back, and John could hear the rasp of fear in his voice as he fell back into his ceaseless, whispered prayers.

In the sudden silence, broken only by distant shouts from the other boats, John could hear the sound of his own heart beating. He tried to still his breath, listening for any sudden swish of water, any splashing that would mean the whale was attacking.

The abrupt hissing of a whale's breech made

them all explode into motion again. John jerked to face starboard. There it was. It rose, water streaming down its dark skin. John could see the rounded squid-scars that dappled most sperm whales' hides. Its blunt head and the off-center blowhole looked unreal to John, as always. God had made his oddest creature in the sperm whale. Its misplaced jaw opened, and John could see the rows of pegged teeth and the ridged flesh that roofed its mouth.

"Oars forward," came Mr. Adams's harsh command. "Pull hard, boys!"

Staring as the whale slid back beneath the water, John lost his grip on his left oar. He struggled to regain it as Mr. Adams bellowed orders, directing the chase. John could not take his eyes from the massive dark form in the water less than a ship's length away. For a long moment, the enormous animal lay still, as though it expected no harm from the little boat racing toward it.

"Harpooner?" Mr. Adams demanded.

John glanced over his shoulder to see Boston George standing up in the bow. The sun glinted on the wicked curves of his broad-bladed harpoon. Stout rope was affixed to it, close to the metal barb.

"To my count!" Mr. Adams roared.

John twisted back around, bracing his feet and dragging at his oar. Mr. Adams was steering hard to port, then he straightened the boat again.

"Rest oars!" Boston George shrieked, and Mr. Adams shouted the order. John, in perfect time with all the others, lifted his oars from the water.

An instant later, John heard a sickening, wet, thudding sound and knew that the first harpoon had been thrown.

"Hit him again!" Mr. Adams was shouting.

John heard a second wrenching thump, then the sound of the coil of rope hissing as it played out over the side of the boat. He held his breath, waiting for the next command from Mr. Adams. From this instant onward, anything could happen and he knew it.

The whale could go deep—the old-timers said no other sea animal could go deeper than a sperm whale. Or it might head for open water and drag them along with it. Or it could turn on them and kill them all.

Time seemed to stop, and John turned to see Boston George shading his eyes, standing clear of the whooshing ropes, gazing down into the water. He stepped back a few seconds before the first rope ran out and snapped taut against its iron ring.

The effect on the boat was immediate. As though a giant hand had caught at its keel, the boat shuddered, then yawed and began to move through the water.

"Set oars," Mr. Adams shouted, and John lowered his oars into the water, leaning against them to add as much resistance as he could. The whale was hurt. If they could exhaust it as well, it might die before it dragged them to kingdom come. Looking over his shoulder, John saw Boston George setting his floats on the ropes. If the whale felt the added burden, it didn't show it. The boat kept moving steadily over the water.

"Nantucket sleigh ride," John heard Mr. Jackson mutter, and he almost smiled at the old-fashioned expression for being dragged by a whale. Then his worries closed in again. Sometimes boats were hauled so far from their ship that they were lost at sea.

A round of shouts made John turn back. The Salazars were in trouble. Their whale, a huge bull by the look of it, was coming out of the water, its trapdoor jaw open wide. It battered the side of the boat with its head, then fell across it as the oarsmen jumped into the sea to avoid being crushed. Antonio stood wide-legged, a harpoon over his head. He brought it down with a whip-like motion that encompassed his whole body, then released it and dove backward as the whale arched away from the sudden pain, churning the water into white foam.

"Drag him!"

John swallowed hard, turning back to face Mr. Adams, then lowered his oars into the water again, bracing himself against the pull. He heard Mr. Jackson's low moan and glanced over his shoulder to see the older man's grimace of strain.

John set his jaw and ground his teeth together, angling his oars until the weight of their resistance was almost more than he could stand. He stared at Mr. Adams, holding on with all his strength. As he watched, the first mate pushed his own long oar straight off the stern, then angled it slowly to port, swinging the boat off to one side. Then, working patiently and steadily, he moved it back, causing the boat to swing the other way.

John knew what he was doing. The harpoons were in deep. Changing the direction of the boat would mean changing the direction of pull on the rope. It would widen the wounds and increase the whale's bleeding.

But in spite of Mr. Adams's constant efforts, the whale did not seem to weaken. The pressure on John's oar did not lessen, and they were pulled farther and farther away from the ship. John began to wish that the whale could live, that it could somehow escape as a reward for its bravery. But that was unlikely, and he knew it.

"How long can he stay down?" John asked quietly, not really expecting an answer, but Mr. Garner shot him a look over his shoulder and laughed.

"I've heard whalers talk about dives that went on close to an hour."

John felt his stomach tighten, but he said no more as the distant form of the ship shrank. The sun sparkled off the water. He tried to stop staring at the diminishing shape of the *Vigilance* but he couldn't.

"Up she comes!" Mr. Garner shouted just as John felt a sudden slackening in the pressure on his oar. An instant later, the sperm whale's blunt head rose into sight, casting a shadow that enveloped the boat. Its odd-shaped mouth gaped open as reddish water streamed from its back.

John leaned backward involuntarily, awed, as he had been every time, by the size and strength of the whale. It fell sideways, and the water sprang up like a fountain, nearly swamping the boat. John reached for the bucket nearest him and began to bail.

The whale came up again, rolling over this time, winding the rope around itself. The boat was jerked forward, the bow dipping low enough to take on more water.

"Bail away, John," Mr. Adams ordered, then gave the command to cut the lines.

Out of the corner of his eye, John saw
Boston George pull his knife from the sheath at
his waist. But before he could reach the ropes,
the whale was diving again, and the boat spun.
John fell sideways, reaching out to grab Mr.
Jackson's shirttail as the old man lost his footing. The boat tipped again, this time to the
other side. Someone screamed.

The water was violent, thrashing like a live
thing beneath the boat. Boston George struggled to his feet, and John saw him reach out
once more with his knife.

"Bail, John!" Mr. Adams ordered.

John scooped the bucket along the bottom
of the boat, pitching water over the side. He
kept his head down as long as he could stand it.
When he glanced up again, he saw Boston
George pointing at the dark water. "Here she
comes. She's up again!"

John steeled himself, laying the bucket down
to grip his oars again. But this time, the whale
rose quietly, sluggishly, bobbing close to the
surface without fighting the ropes still draped
across its back.

"Haul in!" Mr. Adams commanded.

John dipped his oars in the water and took the first stroke alone. By the second, Mr. Garner and Mr. Jackson were timed with him. By the third, Mr. Forbes had joined in, and the boat moved forward.

As they drew closer to the whale, John held his breath. He could hear Boston George praying louder. Mr. Adams made his way forward, stepping over the benches and bending down to pick up the lance that had been stowed with the harpoons. He walked to the bow and lifted the lance high. "Easy now, lads," he said.

John and the others rowed with shallow, slow strokes, stopping when Mr. Adams raised one hand. There was a terrible stillness that seemed to last forever. Then Mr. Adams plunged the lance downward. It sank past the thin blackish skin, through the thick layers of blubber, deep into the whale's lungs. Mr. Adams threw his whole weight against the lance, furiously working the sharpened point back and forth. Then, he pulled it free and bellowed out a chain of orders. "Cut loose! Stern all! Be quick now!"

John fell to rowing, his hands shaking so hard, he could barely keep his grip. It took five or six strokes for them to find a rhythm. By then, the whale had begun its flurry—the final frenzied struggle that could end only in its death.

Rowing hard, they managed to stay clear of the pain-crazed animal. John watched, unable to look away. He cheered with the others when the mighty animal finally floated to the surface and lay still—but his heart was heavy. Even the thought of the bounty he had earned couldn't completely erase the sadness that he always felt as a whale gasped once or twice more, then died.

It took a long time to salvage the mess of rope that circled the whale, and a half hour to tie the gigantic flukes to the stern of the boat. Then they ran the lines forward to the bow so the enormous weight would not simply pull the boat apart.

Towing the massive creature was hard work, and slow, but for John the worst part was the uneasy feeling that always plagued him when he was in the small boat. The ocean stretched away as far as anyone could see in every direction. The whale had pulled them so far that it seemed they were completely alone, bobbing like a tiny acorn.

Mr. Adams set the course, using his compass, and they rowed in shifts—three men working while three rested. Even Mr. Adams took his turn. When the silhouette of the *Vigilance* finally came into sight, John led the cheer.

CHAPTER FOUR

Rebecca stood at the stern railing. Mr. Stevenson was at the helm since Papa had decided to displace him as boat header. His face was impassive, but Rebecca saw him glancing downward at broken oars floating next to the shattered boards that had been a boat a half hour before.

Rebecca hated it when any of the men got hurt. At least Papa was all right. He had abandoned chasing a whale to come back and pull the screaming men from the water. Most of them seemed all right and had climbed the ladders easily enough.

But Mr. Greene—a big, jolly man who always sang at his work—was being raised from

Papa's boat with ropes, like a barrel from a loading dock. His sleeve was bloodied, and as the crew swung the book inward, Rebecca could see that his eyes were closed.

"Clara," Papa called to Mama as the other men steadied Mr. Greene on the deck and loosed his rope harness. "See what you can do for this one."

Mama pointed at the deckhouse. "Lay him on the floor inside." Then she looked up. "Rebecca? Fetch some clean water and bring the ragbag. We are in need of a bandage."

Rebecca hurried toward the copper water tank that sat just in front of the mizzenmast. The ladle was deep and wide, and she filled the small oaken bucket very quickly. She gathered her skirts in one hand and lifted the bucket in the other.

"Set it here," Mama said the moment Rebecca ducked into the deckhouse door.

Mr. Greene's bulky frame took up the entire center of the little room. Rebecca had to step over his legs to position the bucket between the divan and her mother's potted ivy. Then she rushed out, running around the deckhouse to the stairway. She hurried past the horsehair sofa, turning into their stateroom. Mama kept all her yard goods in her trunk. A moment later, Rebecca was on her way back abovedecks, the ragbag swinging from her hand.

Coming around the corner, Rebecca looked out over the water. Papa's boat had drawn away fast. Rebecca knew they were hoping to catch up to the whale they had lost.

Mama was bent over Mr. Greene now, her face grim and tight. She looked up. "Sort through the bag, Rebecca. Pull out anything that's got enough length to it."

Rebecca sank to her knees, glancing sidelong at Mr. Greene's arm as Mama dribbled water on it to wash away the blood. There was something jutting up out of the wound, something white.

"Have you found a piece of cloth that will do?" Mama asked, her voice clipped and precise.

Rebecca shook her head and looked back down into the bag of scraps, trembling. "Here," she said, pulling out a long piece of white dimity. It had been the hemline of an old dress of Mama's she had shortened for Rebecca the year before.

"That'll do," Mama said as she took it. "And ask Joseph to send the fourth mate to assist me, please."

Rebecca could not stop glancing at the jagged hole in Mr. Greene's arm and the odd white of his exposed bone.

"Rebecca!"

She stood up, leaving the ragbag beside her mother, and turned, hurrying back out onto the deck. She finally spotted her brother. He was helping coil rope. "Joseph!" she called. He looked up. "Is Mr. Potter there?"

"I am here, Miss."

Rebecca looked to port and saw the thin young man her father had made fourth mate when Mr. Hendersen had run off in Lahaina. Mr. Potter had dark, sincere eyes and Rebecca liked him. "Mama needs your help."

Mr. Potter nodded gravely. "I wondered if she might." He stepped past, and Rebecca watched him go, then looked out to sea, watching her father's boat as it moved farther away from the ship. What if Papa ever got badly hurt?

A speck, almost too small to see, caught Rebecca's eye. She stared at it fixedly until she could see the flash of the oars in the sun. When Mr. Potter called for a crewman's help, Rebecca turned to watch them walk Mr. Greene slowly across the deck, then down the forward hatch. Mr. Greene staggered from side to side, cradling his bandaged arm.

"They have a whale!" Joseph piped up from his position in the bow. "Mr. Adams has a whale!"

Rebecca looked back over the railing. He was right. The boat was towing a huge carcass behind it. She could hear the mate calling to his oarsmen and recognized Mr. Adams's voice. She exhaled slowly, looking heavenward, grateful that Mr. Adams and his crew were all right.

Major! Rebecca whirled around. She had forgotten all about him in the confusion. Almost running, she ducked into the deckhouse. Mama was sitting in Papa's chair, her face in her hands. Instead of asking about Major,

Rebecca went to stand beside her mother. "Are you all right, Mama?"

Mama looked up. "I will be. Where is Joseph?"

"Still up coiling the ropes."

"Can you see your father's boat?"

Rebecca nodded. "And Mr. Adams's boat is coming in with a big one."

Mama's face brightened, and she stood to go out on deck. Rebecca glanced around the deckhouse. "Have you seen Major?"

Mama sighed. "He's down in the after-cabin, curled up on your father's horsehair couch, useless animal that he is."

"Mr. Hawkins said he caught a rat in the pantry yesterday," Rebecca protested.

Mama only shook her head. "Stop worrying over that cat and say a prayer for your papa," she said quietly. "And Mr. Greene."

Rebecca nodded, lowering her head. She said the prayers silently. She knew that the sooner they had enough oil, the sooner Papa would start home, but she also wished that they would never see a whale again. Seven men had died in the three years they had been at sea. Mr. Greene might die, too, if his wound went sour.

The sound of shouting made Rebecca look up. "Let's go see them as they come in," Mama said. "This will be the last breath of fresh air we have for days."

Rebecca nodded. The trying out always meant clouds of greasy black smoke hanging over the boat. She followed Mama back out onto the deck. They stood, looking off the starboard side as the boat approached. It was a big whale. The small boat and the men inside it looked tiny next to the dead goliath.

"Joseph!" Mama called out. He looked up, then ducked his head. "Come on, now," Mama called. "Out of the way." Joseph hesitated a second or two longer, then obeyed.

"Come alongside!" Rebecca heard Mr. Adams shout.

She stepped up to the rail to watch just as Joseph came up, his eyes bright with excitement. "Mama, do you see how big it is?" he asked breathlessly.

Rebecca saw her mother nod, then look

back out at the huge carcass that the men were securing to the starboard side. It was a process that always amazed her, no matter how many times she had seen it done.

The men maneuvered the boat around so that the whale lay alongside the ship. Rising and falling gently with the motion of the sea, the huge carcass was held still while the heavy chains were lowered and passed beneath it, just below its long, strangely shaped jaw. Then the winches were manned. As the crewmen heaved on the long handles, the head of the whale rose out of the water, its body slanting downward.

The men aboard cheered as the cutting stage was lowered to within an arm's length of the water. Rebecca saw John and three other men step out of the boat onto the platform.

"Cutting spades, coming down," a crewman shouted, and Rebecca watched as the tools were passed to the men on the platform. They stood on the narrow planking, talking in voices too low for Rebecca to hear, but she could imagine what they were saying. Their job was to reduce the body of the whale to barrels of oil. They were deciding which of them would make the first cuts.

John and the older man named Mr. Jackson were elected to cut off the whale's head. They often did difficult tasks together. Rebecca knew, from eavesdropping on her father's conversations with Mr. Adams, that he believed in pairing experience with youth anytime the opportunity presented itself. Most captains did.

Mr. Jackson began by leaning out and slicing a shallow cut in the whale's black skin, showing the young freedman where to begin. Then work commenced.

The sounds from the cutting spades were sickening, but Rebecca, as always, could not seem to look away. It took a long time for the two men to sever the whale's head. Once they had, more chains were lowered, and huge hooks were set into the ragged flesh. Straining, all hands helped haul the massive head inboard. Joseph let out a whoop as it swung inward and the crew settled it on deck, next to the brick rectangle of the tryworks.

Rebecca turned to watch as the Salazar

brothers were lowered to stand on the platform beside the carcass. While they shouted back and forth in Portuguese, figuring out where to begin the cutting in, John and Mr. Jackson were brought up on deck.

Rebecca saw John grinning at the older man as they approached the head. It was a tradition on Papa's ships for men whose boat crews had killed a whale to be among those who emptied the finest oil from its case.

Rebecca glanced toward the bow and saw Mr. Garner and Mr. Forbes climbing over the bulwark and stepping onto the deck. Mr. Forbes took the cutting spade that was offered to him and climbed up the ladder to open the whale's head. Sliding down inside the cut, he used a drill to make a big hole in the thick bone of the immense skull.

Young John was given the dubious honor of bailing out the precious oil that filled the strange, fleshy tank inside the whale's skull. Rebecca watched him for a long time as he brought out bucketful after bucketful, handing them down, then grabbing empties from

Mr. Forbes, who now stood on the ladder.

Mr. Nilsen was busy directing the men who rolled empty barrels up the companionway from his workshop belowdecks and set them alongside the whale's head. Once each one was filled with the clear, warm oil, a second crew topped them and wrestled them down into the hold, where they would stay until the ship reached New Bedford again.

Rebecca wrinkled her nose as she smelled the first wisps of wood smoke. The men were starting the fires in the brick tryworks. She looked over the rail. The Salazar brothers both held broad, cutting spades. They leaned outward, jabbing the wide, razor-sharp blades straight down, through the whale's thin black skin into the thick layer of blubber. Their jabs made long, parallel cuts, an arm's length wide, as far across the whale's bobbing body as they could.

Watching the next step had been hard for Rebecca at first, but now, she was used to it. A huge iron hook was lowered as the Salazars, working together, dug down beneath their previous scarf cuts, lifting a strip of blubber. They used a lance to pierce the strip. Then Mr. O'Neille was lowered on a rope. He worked the sharpened hook through the pierced hole and yelled to the men above, who began to turn the long-handled windlass. It raised a pair of long boards that crossed the main mast, working like a giant seesaw. As the windlass lines pulled one end down, the end attached to the blubber hook was lifted.

Taking turns now, the Salazars hacked at the base of the blanket strip, freeing it inch by inch as the windlass pulled it upward. The whale's body turned slowly as they worked, continuing the spiral cut along the body. At intervals the Salazars would cut through the strip, and each segment would be hauled inboard and swung onto the deck. Then they started over, working side by side.

"Joseph! You get down from there."

At the sound of her mother's voice, Rebecca turned and saw her brother perched in the rigging, his swinging feet just out of Mama's reach.

"I want to see the sharks when they come," Joseph answered. "Papa let me do it last time."

"Not another hairsbreadth higher," Mama warned. Joseph nodded happily and turned his face back toward the ocean.

On deck, men were chopping up the blubber where it lay, next to the huge head. John was finishing up at bailing, Rebecca saw, and reaching for the long, hoelike tool that he would use to scrape out the spermaceti from the lower part of the skull. Most of it would be sold to candle makers, but some would end up in cosmetic pomades and salves, sitting on marble dressing tables next to fine perfumes and silver hairbrushes.

Rebecca wondered how fancy women could use the cheek-rouge and salves that were made from the waxy stuff. They probably had no idea where it came from. Spermaceti didn't stink, but if those women would even once smell the stench of a trying out, or see the ugly process of scraping the whale's junk, they would likely find prettier sources for their cosmetics.

"Joseph!" Mama shouted over the din of creaking winches and shouting men. Rebecca looked upward. Her brother was creeping higher. She looked out at sea and saw the ruddy color of the bloody water spreading outward from the whale's carcass.

When she turned back, Rebecca saw that the first blanket strip of blubber had been cut into horse pieces now. The men had spread out on the greasy deck, and their cutting spades flashed in the sunlight. The horse pieces were laid out, skin side down, then sliced into thin, pagelike sections—with the black skin still attached. The men called these "bible leaves" because they looked like opened books when they were done.

The bible leaves were carried to the try-pots by the four or five men who weren't helping with the cutting up. Rebecca grimaced as the air began to carry the pungent stink of boiling blubber.

She looked out to sea again, then glanced at her mother. There were clouds roiling up far to the south now. Mama caught her glance and nodded. "Your father will be back well before any weather has time to come in."

Rebecca nodded and turned in time to see John helping to cut free the lower jaw. Mr. Jackson was bent over the grooved jawbone. He was running his hands over the fine-grained ivory of the huge, flattopped teeth. He was smiling.

"Mr. Bellamy astern! He has a whale!" someone cried out.

Rebecca turned to see the third mate's boat approaching. The hands on deck raised a cheer. She turned in a circle, looking for Papa's boat. It was not yet in sight.

CHAPTER FIVE

Early the next morning, a freshet of spray spattered cold salt water across John's face. He opened his eyes. It had been a long night. The captain's boat had finally returned with all safe, but no whale.

He rubbed at his eyes. The wind had come up. It was midmorning, but he had no idea what time it might be. When the try-pots were boiling, the shifts ran together, every man working as many hours as he could until the job was done.

John stretched. He had slept only a few hours, but he felt better for it. Boat crews were forgiven a little sleep, so long as there were enough men working to keep the barrels filling.

He blinked and looked toward the tryworks. The wind was blowing the thick, greasy smoke toward the port side.

John winced at the stink and squeezed his eyes shut to dull the ache. If it didn't get too strong, the wind would be a godsend. Usually, the smoke hung in a thick, choking cloud over the deck. John's eyes often hurt for three or four days after the try-pot fires were put out. The smoke was acrid.

John stared upward at the sails, listening to the raucous sounds of the gulls. There would be dozens of birds flying close to the ship now. They always came around when whales had been killed. Even the goneys would stay close, circling on their huge, unmoving wings for days on end. They would swoop down to gorge themselves on floating pieces of scrap that was thrown overboard from the try-pots. A nimbus of grease and blood surrounded the boat. Birds would be plentiful for a few days.

John felt the ship rocking beneath him. The flat calm of the past few days was over. High in the sky, wisps of white clouds were scattered.

The wind whistled lightly through the rigging overhead. Captain Whittier had ordered half the canvas lowered, content to sail slowly while they were busy at the tryworks.

John turned onto his side, easing the aches in his legs from the hard deck planks. He had slept on deck because he had no other place to sleep. Russell was in the bunk—he needed it; he was hurt pretty bad. Mrs. Whittier had wrapped the exposed bone, Fourth Mate Potter had said. John knew the wound could easily sour.

John looked heavenward and tried to remember a prayer to recite. When he couldn't, he made up a short one, but felt silly doing it. Why would God listen to him? He and his father almost never went to church—and he almost never prayed. He wished he could now. He liked Russell.

Maybe today, John thought, he could get Mr. Hawkins to give him some meat broth to spoon up for Russell. He hadn't talked much the last time John had gone down to look in on him. He had been flushed, and his eyes were half closed. But he had asked not to be left out when it came time to fry up doughnuts in the last few pots of oil. John hoped that was a good sign—Russell had always loved the doughnuts.

John saw Captain Whittier's family standing to one side of the deckhouse. Joseph was facing his mother, an expression of exaggerated petulance on his face. He was likely arguing to be allowed to help out with the try-pots. He loved to shovel the boiled-out scrap blubber into the fires. The smoke stank horribly, but the flames leaped high.

John hoped Captain Whittier would keep Joseph away. There was no room for boyish foolishness around the tryworks, especially if the seas were going to pick up like this. Spilled oil was dangerous. More than one ship had been set afire and burned to the waterline.

John stood up, pulling his coat closed against the chill of the stiff breeze. It was hard to sleep on deck when it was this cold. He looked starboard, leaning a little to see around the broad base of the mizzenmast. Miss Whittier was standing, as she so often did, with her black-and-white cat in her arms. If it got away from her today, John thought, smiling, its pampered black-and-white fur would get greasy.

Miss Whittier's hair had escaped her bonnet and was blowing across her face. She freed one hand to push it back from her brow. The cat saw its chance and leaped to the deck, but she caught it up again. John hid his smile and turned before Captain Whittier noticed. He would not allow a crewman to stare at his daughter.

John walked along the bulwark, toward the tryworks, his eyes on the dancing flames. Even the deck aft, where he had slept, was greasy. Closer to the boiling pots where slabs of blubber were being cut up, it was awash with the thick, slippery oil and shreds of spermaceti.

"Forbes could use a hand down on the platform!" John looked up to see Mr. Jackson's nearly toothless grin. "Sharks. Captain says he'll pay two dollars' extra wages to anyone who'll help."

John nodded and reluctantly made his way to the starboard rail. He looked downward. They had finished trying out the big sperm bull. Now, the smaller whale that Mr. Bellamy's crew had killed was chained to the side of the ship. They hadn't done too badly. Four spotted and two killed.

Two men from the first shift were working: Rory O'Neille, and a Shinnecock Indian everyone called Charlie Shell because of a necklace he wore. They were gutting the whale. John watched them lifting the huge coils of intestine. Charlie Shell was the best cutter onboard, Russell said.

Maybe they would find ambergris. He hoped so. It was very valuable and would increase the lay. John knew he would be lucky to clear his father's debt to Mr. Tildon this time out. If he did have to go out again, he wanted to be a ship's mate. The officers, even the lower ranks, got much bigger shares of the lay.

John looked past Mr. O'Neille and Charlie Shell. Mr. Forbes was standing aft, lance in hand. The water was choppy, roughened by the wind. The platform itself was swinging in rhythm with the ship's rise and fall. The water was dark with whale's blood. John steadied himself, then glanced up. There were winks of lightning on the southern horizon now.

John opened the locker that held the harpoons and lances. The first row was all special—weapons that belonged to members of the crew and were only stored here. The second row was ship's property. John chose a long-handled lance and tested the tip on his index finger. It was sharp, and the head seemed tight in the haft.

Hefting the lance in his right hand, John looked longingly toward the forward hatch. What he really wanted was breakfast, but he knew he wasn't likely to get it now. He squared his shoulders. At least he was missing a meal for a good reason. Two dollars' extra would pay for his next shirt from the slop chest.

John skirted a deep puddle of grease that had settled along the bulwark and made his way to the rope-ladder that led down to the cutting stage. The planks were wet, and John was careful to time his first step onto the stage precisely. He stood still for a few seconds, getting used to the swinging motion.

"John! Look sharp!"

Turning, John saw Mr. Forbes glaring at him.

He stood on the far side of the cutters, a lance in his hand. As John watched, a stiff, triangular fin knifed through the water, moving past him. Mr. Forbes raised the lance and struck downward. He jerked the lance back, freeing the slender iron tip, then struck downward again. Within an instant, there were two more fins circling the wounded shark.

Charlie Shell glanced up. "Jackson was supposed to come."

John shook his head. "He told me to—"

"You be careful, then, little John. Strike quick, then move back." Charlie Shell mimed the technique.

John nodded, grateful as always that at least some of the older men were willing to teach him the skills he needed to make it home alive. He braced his feet and turned to face out toward the open ocean. He saw a fin almost immediately and watched the shark approach, circling away, then coming closer again. Ignoring the shouted conversation of the others, he stared at the slick gray fin and stood waiting, his lance raised.

John held the lance as steady as he could, plunging it downward with all his strength, then jerking it back toward himself. The swing of the platform made him stumble, and for a long, terrifying second, he was afraid he would pitch forward into the water. Then, Charlie Shell turned and reversed his cutting spade, jabbing the long handle toward John. John clutched at it, steadying himself.

"Keep your footing," Charlie Shell warned him. "Don't use the lance until you are braced."

John nodded, his heart pounding as the water just in front of him exploded into motion. There was a tight circling of gray fins that churned up an ugly pink foam. John heard Mr. Forbes laugh aloud as the sharks turned on one of their number and began to feed.

John moved away, placing his feet carefully. He had seen one man attacked by sharks. No one who had ever seen how fierce the big gray fish could be ever needed to be warned about them again.

"More coming," Mr. Forbes sang out.

John set his feet, then struck at a shark that

swam close. It writhed in the water and turned toward him, its razor teeth slashing in vain. The platform was just high enough that most sharks didn't understand where the enemy was, John knew. But he had heard stories of men being dragged down into the water.

"Look away astern," Mr. Forbes shouted.

John turned to see two more sharks closing in. He swallowed hard and raised the lance. It was almost impossible to kill a shark this way, but that didn't seem to matter. Once they were bleeding, the others attacked them.

"Cut away quick as you can," Mr. Adams shouted from the rail. "Storm's coming!" Charlie Shell shouted an acknowledgment.

John glanced up. The clouds were thickening and spreading. It would not be long before the sun was covered. There was a wheeling circle of gulls in the sky above the ship.

A drenching spray of cold water startled John into turning. Less than an arm's reach away, three or four sharks were snatching mouthfuls of the whale's exposed flesh. Mr. O'Neille cursed and grabbed a hoist chain to steady himself as the carcass beneath his feet quivered under the onslaught.

John jabbed at a flash of shiny gray skin, then widened his stance and waited. There were eight or ten sharks now, swimming beneath the surface, appearing and disappearing as they circled.

Mr. O'Neille dragged another section of the whale's guts free, and he and Charlie Shell set to work cutting them open, looking for ambergris. John only glanced at them, then looked back at the water. It was boiling with the movement of the sharks. Charlie Shell and Mr. O'Neille gathered a pile of intestine between them, then leaned to drop it into the water.

As John watched, all the sharks seemed to dive at once. Then there was a quiet moment, and John heard the cries of the seabirds, flying low, fighting over scraps.

Suddenly, the whale carcass shook violently. Charlie Shell stepped calmly from the whale's belly onto the cutting stage. "Rory!" he shouted. "That's it. Cut it loose." He gestured with his cutting spade, indicating the shark-churned water.

Mr. O'Neille was hanging on to the hoist chain with both hands, unable to find secure footing. He had buried the blade of his cutting spade in the carcass, and it stuck up awkwardly. He nodded to show he had heard, then struggled forward far enough to jerk the cutting tool free. "John!" he shouted, then gave the spade a careful toss.

John reached out to catch it and slid sideways on the wet planks. He fell hard, his right leg dropping down into the water. Frantic, he knocked the spade aside, barely managing to keep hold of his lance. He scrambled back to his feet just as a shark nosed up out of the water where his right leg had dangled a moment before. Charlie Shell shouted in relief, and John grinned at him, still shaking from the close call.

John stared at the slanted, barely floating handle of the cutting spade, his elation fading. If he lost the tool, he'd have to pay for it. Turning his lance around, he reached out and nudged the spade closer. The iron blade was heavy. The thick, blunt end of the handle kept dipping below the water's surface.

John worked it closer, trying to lift it up with his lance tip, but it only slid deeper. He stared it, then looked up. Charlie Shell was safe on the platform, and Mr. O'Neille had climbed onto one of the rope-ladders that hung down the side of the ship.

"Raise the stage!" Mr. O'Neille was shouting to the deckhands.

John felt the planks quiver beneath his feet and knew this was his last chance. He tucked his lance beneath his left arm and then squatted, gripping the low rail. He could still see the submerged handle. He took a deep breath, scanning the water for gray fins, then plunged his hand in, pulling the cutting spade out. Then he stood, flinching backward as the water stirred and he could see the dull gleam of sharks' teeth.

CHAPTER SIX

Rebecca dreaded the sound of the rising wind. She had seen much worse weather, but the decks were slimy with oil and the tryworks still held blazing fires. Papa had stationed men around the deck to beat out wind-borne sparks.

"Come inside!" Mama called from beside the deckhouse.

Rebecca pretended not to hear, pushing her tangled hair back beneath her bonnet. She wanted to turn and tell her mother to be careful not to let Major slink past, but that would mean letting on that she had indeed heard— and once she admitted that, she would have to obey. She hated being belowdecks when the sea was high. As scared as she sometimes felt standing on the deck, it was a hundred times worse in the small room below.

"Joseph!"

Rebecca looked past the companionway to spot her brother. He was standing with Charlie Shell, watching for sparks. Charlie liked Joseph and often let him help with simple tasks. Mama said Charlie missed his own children.

Rebecca counted to fifteen, then twenty, then forced herself to keep going up to one hundred before she risked a glance back toward the deckhouse. Mama had gone inside to finish mixing up the first batch of dough. Rebecca wondered if Papa would even let them fry the doughnuts. The men would be sorely disappointed if he didn't. But they were probably too tired to start fights or cause too much trouble.

Rebecca shivered a little in the wind. It wasn't really cold, but there was a penetrating dampness in the air. She knew she should go help her mother, but she didn't want to. Just for once, she wanted to be able to walk around.

"Rebecca!"

It was Papa's voice, and he sounded angry. She spun around. "Yes, Papa?"

"Aren't you supposed to be helping your mother?"

Rebecca lowered her eyes. "Yes, Papa."

He frowned. "The men have been looking forward to eating something besides salt pork and hardtack for nearly a month."

"What about the wind?" Rebecca asked.

He shrugged. "We saw worse wind coming around the cape and tried out three whales in the middle of all that, remember?"

Rebecca nodded as her father walked past. He was right. They had. And she and Mama had been scared all night long that the blowing sparks would ignite the grease-soaked decks. She looked forward and saw John Lowe climbing inboard, stepping over the bulwark. He was carrying a lance.

"Rebecca!"

Startled, she looked at her father, then gathered up her skirts and hurried around the side of the deckhouse. She ducked down the stairs and went in, closing the door immediately behind herself. Major was curled up on the long sofa, and she stopped a moment to pet him. He was half asleep. The rocking of the ship never seemed to bother him at all.

Rebecca went through the door into the forward cabin. Mama was bent over her biggest tin pot. The flour sack stood against the wall. She looked up. "There you are. Just in time to give me a rest." She held out the long-handled spoon.

Rebecca took it and stepped forward, lurching a little to one side as the ship rolled. Mama moved out of her way and leaned on the Scotchman's table.

The batter was stiff, and Rebecca had to use two hands to move the spoon through the thick flour-and-water mixture. Over the smell of the saleratus and the wet flour, she could smell the sweet odor of cinnamon and looked up at her mother in surprise.

"I thought we all needed a little something special this afternoon," Mama said.

Rebecca couldn't help but smile. "You'll have the Irishers calling you a saint, Mama."

"I intend to carry them right on out, too. If we wait, the wind may stop us. I only hope your father doesn't mind." Mama captured a stray strand of hair and tucked it beneath her bonnet. "It just seems like all their hard work deserves something more than a stormy night in greasy clothes."

Rebecca worked at the heavy batter. She was used to seeing the little worms that had infested the flour, but they still made her feel queasy. She put all of her strength into stirring and, within a few minutes, had finished the job her mother had started. The batter was smooth and shiny. Rebecca straightened up.

"Help me carry the tin out to the try-pots now, Rebecca," Mama said.

"But they aren't—"

"I am hoping they will empty the blubber from at least one of the pots, and we can get a start on this before the storm gets too bad."

Rebecca waited for her mother to get the skimmer from its hook in her cutlery chest; then they lifted the heavy tin between them, struggling up the narrow stairs.

* * *

John had helped cut up the last of the blubber. Now, he was so hungry that his stomach seemed to be collapsing in on itself. When he spotted Mrs. Whittier and her daughter coming past the deckhouse carrying the big tin basin between them, his heart leaped. Doughnuts!

No sooner had he thought it than old Mr. Jackson shouted out the word for everyone to hear. All hands turned to watch as Mrs. Whittier and her daughter approached. A cheer erupted from the men.

Captain Whittier went to stand beside his wife. She looked up into his face, saying something that was lost in the shouting. After a few seconds, the Captain lifted the tin basin himself and carried it close to the tryworks. Yelling orders, he sent Mr. Hawkins scuttling below and set four men to mopping away the thick layer of grease around the brick base of the tryworks. Mr. Hawkins reappeared, carrying one of the enormous flat trays he used in the galley. Within minutes, a path had been cleared, and Mr. Hawkins had pulled the last of the scrap from one try-pot, leaving only the clear oil bubbling and seething.

Mrs. Whittier quickly took her place by the huge caldron. Her daughter approached more cautiously. A loose half-circle of crewmen formed around them. John's mouth began to water as he watched Mrs. Whittier ladle the sticky dough into the oil. When the faint scent of cinnamon drifted toward him, tears sprang into his eyes. The odor brought back the memory of his mother's kitchen. He closed his eyes and said a prayer for her good health, lifting his chin and raising his face heavenward.

"Psssssssst! Young John? You hide some for me?"

John opened his eyes and saw Antonio Salazar peering at him from his lookout's perch in the rigging. The man's stern, scowling face was intent. His eyes kept flickering back to where Mrs. Whittier stood.

John nodded. Antonio always tried to get more than his share of whatever food there was. And he was big enough and mean enough that no one wanted to cross him.

"Do you hear me, boy?" Antonio demanded.

John nodded, a slight motion that no one else would notice. "I will."

Antonio stared at him a moment more before he looked back out to sea, squinting against the late afternoon sun. John stepped forward, scanning the circle of wolfish faces. Antonio would hold him to his word.

Mr. Hawkins leaned forward, and John could hear men on both sides of him pull in a quick, anticipatory breath as the cook leaned close, examined the frying dough. The men who were still cutting up the last of the blubber paused in their work. Mr. Hawkins shook his head, and the men went back to their tasks.

John looked up at the sky. It was clear to the west where the sun was, but south and east, the clouds had thickened, and the winks of lightning were brighter.

A sudden shuffling of feet made John look back at the caldron. Mr. Hawkins had taken the skimmer from Mrs. Whittier's hand and was lifting out steaming-hot, potato-shaped lumps of the fried dough. The smell of spice thickened, and John's mouth flooded with saliva.

"Second watch goes to the galley first," Captain Whittier called out.

John's whole body reacted to the captain's words. He joined the stampede toward the forward hatch as Mr. Hawkins lifted the tray and headed toward the main companionway. Mrs. Whittier, with her daughter holding the tin steady against the rocking of the ship, began to spoon more dough into the try-pot.

John looked back as Captain Whittier moved closer to the cauldron and faced the ring of men. "First watch, man your stations. Keep the barrels moving toward the hold. Any free, stay close to the tryworks. Every man alert for fire!"

John went down the steep steps, keeping pace with the others. As they all passed through the forecastle, John looked into his bunk. Russell was lying with his face to the wall. John decided not to disturb him. He ducked beneath the huge beam above the galley door and smelled the cinnamon again.

"Take three, no more," Mr. Hawkins was saying as the men pressed close to the head table.

The tray was stacked high with the gold-brown doughnuts. John fell in behind Mr. Jackson and waited his turn.

"Take three," Mr. Hawkins kept repeating.

John chose the three largest on the tray and was about to move on when third mate Mr. Bellamy came clattering in with another full batch. John reached for one extra, and Mr. Hawkins cleared his throat loudly.

"They're for Mr. Greene," John said in a low voice.

Mr. Hawkins nodded. "All right, then. If the wind will leave us be, there'll be plenty more. But some will say that Greene can't eat any and I've let you cheat." He leaned close. "Hide that fourth one in your shirt, son."

John nodded, grateful. If he hadn't gotten the extra, he would have had to give up two of his own: one for Russell and one for Mr. Salazar.

John sighed as he left the galley. It was a near-certainty that he would be sleeping in odd corners or abovedecks for a long time. It would be such a luxury at least to sleep on a truly full belly.

The forecastle was crowded again. Men were

sitting on their trunks, stuffing their mouths full, grinning at each other. John tucked two more doughnuts inside his shirt, keeping only one in his hand.

"Russell?" John reached out and gently nudged the sleeping man's shoulder.

Russell groaned and shifted, turning his head. "John, lad. I am glad to see you."

John winced at the misery in Russell's voice. "I only brought one." He held out the dough-nut. Russell's eyes lit. "Captain Whittier might stop the frying if the wind gets worse, so I—"

"Give it here, boy," Russell interrupted. "Explain to me while I'm eating."

John laughed. As Russell chewed slowly, enjoying every crumb, John told him about the trying out, about the storm to the south, and the sharks he had killed.

Russell chuckled, then grimaced, holding his bandaged arm. "I remember when you were enough of a greenie to wonder which side was port."

John shook his head, smiling. It wasn't true. He had followed his blacksmith father onto any number of ships, from the time he was able to help carry tools. But he had known nothing about whaling—that much was a fact.

"I'll bring you more if we get more," John promised.

Russell nodded. "I thank you for the use of the bunk, son. I will repay you somehow."

John nodded. "How's the arm?"

"Hurts like knives and fire," Russell said flatly. "The bone is all smashed up. Maybe it'll heal."

John could only nod. The dim light in the forecastle still showed the spreading red stains on Mrs. Whittier's bandage. About a month before, a crewman had been cut by a mishandled harpoon. He had seemed fine, then had sickened and died in fever in spite of Mr. Pratt's cures and poultices. John blinked, feeling uneasy.

"Go on, then," Russell said. "Get me a couple more if you can."

John nodded again and turned away to climb back abovedecks. The instant his head cleared the shelter of the hatch, John knew the wind was stronger than it had been a few minutes before. The sea was higher, too. The ship was rolling now, breasting small waves. Belowdecks it had felt like a minor swell. Up here, looking at the dark clouds to the south, it looked much worse. The sun was lowering fast.

John climbed up the rigging to hand Antonio his doughnut. He explained that there might not be any more coming.

"Then it is a good thing I asked you this favor," Antonio said, smiling. As he crammed the oily pastry into his mouth, his face took on the same dreamy joy that everyone else's had.

John climbed back down the rigging and stood on deck, looking around. All the blubber was in the try-pots now, and four men were using rope-mops to wash away some of the grease. They had made it just in time.

John smiled and pulled a doughnut out of his shirt. His first bite filled his cheeks like a squirrel's. Everything seemed perfect. They were going to arrive back in New Bedford with a hold full of oil barrels, ambergris, and spermaceti—Mr. Tildon was going to make a lot of money from this voyage. He was known to be more honest than many shipowners, too. That meant he would probably not exaggerate the accounts too much. Some owners charged the men double or more for every shirt, spoon, or pair of boots they had to buy out of the ship's slop chest.

John faced into the wind, chewing happily. If it was going to get bad enough, he wanted to sleep belowdecks. But if it wasn't going to be much of a storm, he preferred the cool, fresh air. John pulled his last doughnut out of his shirt and began to eat it. The ache in his stomach was easing, his hunger dulled.

Glancing at the tryworks, he saw Mrs. Whittier lifting more doughnuts out of the bubbling oil. Captain Whittier stood beside her, saying something that John couldn't hear. He watched them closely, trying to figure out whether or not Captain Whittier was going to make them douse the fires yet. The ship was rolling now, and overhead, the clouds were darkening. Suddenly, lightning crackled through the sky, giving the rigging an eerie blue cast. John hunched his shoulders against the first few drops of rain.

CHAPTER SEVEN

By evening, every timber in the ship was creaking and squealing. Rebecca clung to the edge of her pallet. The heaving of the ship made her a little sick. Mama and Joseph were much worse off, as usual. Mama had taken to her own bed. Joseph lay groaning on his cot.

"Don't close your eyes," Rebecca told him.

He groaned again. "I don't want any more doughnuts. Ever."

Rebecca smiled, knowing he wasn't looking. "It isn't the doughnuts. It's the storm."

Joseph whimpered, one hand over his mouth.

"Rebecca?" Mama called from her bed.

"Yes, Mama."

"Bring a basin in from the after-cabin's cut-lery chest, will you?"

Rebecca knew what Mama was thinking. Joseph was going to throw up. She stood up and started along the wall, reaching out to touch it, then gripping the tall bedpost as she passed her mother's bed. At the doorway she stopped, bracing herself for a few seconds.

"Hurry," Joseph pleaded. Then he groaned again.

Over the high-pitched complaints of the beams, Rebecca could hear her mother weep-ing quietly. Mama hated storms. They made her deathly ill and they scared her. Rebecca was scared, too, but she was lucky and she knew it. She had Papa's stomach, not her mother's. Papa would stand at the helm, his hands on the oak wheel until the storm quieted. Joseph might dream of being a ship's captain, but how would he ever be able to steer the boat in a storm?

Rebecca started forward again, hanging on to the Scotchman's table as she passed it. It was as steady as anything on the ship. The mizzenmast rose straight through the far end of it, and the legs were pegged into the deck.

The cutlery trunk was on the far wall, and Rebecca had to cross the room to get to it. She let go of the edge of the table and took a single step forward, keeping her knees a little bent as Papa had taught her. An abrupt sideways jerk of the deck beneath her feet made Rebecca lurch forward, falling hard on her knees. She bit her lip and managed not to cry out. Mama had enough to worry about.

"Hurry!" Joseph's voice sounded weak.

Rebecca rolled into a sitting position, then tried to stand up again. The floor rose abruptly, and she gasped, then lost her balance when it dropped from beneath her again. She sprawled on the floor again, this time smacking her chin painfully when she hit. Crawling back to the table, she pulled herself upward.

Rebecca eyed the trunk across the room. It was so close, but the heaving of the ship made it seem like an impossible distance. Pulling in a determined breath, she waited until there was an instant's lull. Then she lunged forward, arms extended, and fell across the arched back of the trunk.

The lid was heavy and awkward. Rebecca raised it, keeping her balance by bracing her feet wide apart. She stood peering down into the trunk for a few seconds as the ship slammed into another swell and rose again. Then she reached in and snatched out the basin, afraid the trunk lid would bounce forward and drop on her hands.

Rebecca managed to close the trunk and turn back toward the opposite wall without falling. But it was all she could do to stay upright as the ship was lifted, then crashed down again, listing hard to the port side. Joseph cried out, and she could hear her mother's gasp of fear.

Her heart beating fast, Rebecca made her way, one unsteady step at a time, back to her brother's cot. Bracing herself against the wall with one outstretched hand, she bent to lay the basin beside him. His eyes were shut tight. "Here it is, Joseph."

He said nothing, but raised himself on his

elbows and looked at her, his eyes dull with nausea and fear. "How bad is the storm?"

Rebecca shrugged, trying to sound calm. "I don't know, Joseph. It feels pretty bad."

Joseph wiped at his damp forehead. "Mr. Adams says Papa is the best high seas captain he's ever seen."

Rebecca nodded. "He has brought us through every storm so far," she answered, sounding like Mama, but he didn't seem to notice. She didn't know what else to say. She was scared, too.

The ship rolled, and the floor slanted to starboard. Joseph suddenly clutched at the basin and retched. Rebecca turned away, more nauseated by the sound of her brother's vomiting than by the constant motion of the ship.

When Joseph's retching had stilled, Rebecca forced herself to take the basin. Fighting to keep her balance, she pulled open the door that led to their little water closet and stepped onto the first stair, reaching up to dump the basin just as the ship lurched again. As she turned back, she could hear Joseph throwing up again.

She hurried as much as she could, but the deck pitched beneath her feet and she fell at the foot of Mama's bed. Using the footboard to pull herself up again, she managed to stagger two more steps to Joseph's side. There was no mess on his bedclothes. He had the dry heaves. Rebecca left the basin and went to lie down on her own bed.

"Is your brother all right?" Mama called.

"I think so," Rebecca said. "Are you?"

Mama made a sound of pure misery.

The rising and falling of the ship went on. Mama groaned and wept, and Rebecca had no idea what to do to help her. Joseph's stomach would not settle, and she could hear his exhausted crying in between bouts of nausea.

Time dragged past, and Rebecca got up to trim the lantern wick and to make sure it was steady in its bracket. The oil in the glass was sloshing with the movement of the ship, but not splashing up through the wick slot yet. Rebecca hoped it wouldn't.

The only thing worse than being stuck inside their cabin in bad weather was being

stuck inside it in the dark. But if the ship's toss-
ing got bad enough, they would have to put it
out. The risk of a fire starting would be too
great.

Coming back, Rebecca hesitated beside
Joseph's cot, resisting an urge to touch the back
of his head, to try to comfort him a little. She
had been sick a few times—though never as
bad as this—and all she had wanted was to be
left alone.

"Rebecca?"

Rebecca looked up to see her mother half-
sitting in her bed now. Her face had a sheen of
sweat on it, and there were shadows beneath
her eyes. The creaking of the timbers and the aft
mast seemed to get louder as Rebecca waited
for her mother to swallow, then speak.

"Rebecca, your brother needs an emetic."

Rebecca nodded, glancing at Joseph. There
had been a storm south of the Hawaiian Islands
that had been bad enough to make Joseph
almost as sick as he was now. The steward kept
a chest of medicines down in the galley. He had
given Joseph a draft that had helped.

Mama swung her legs around, resting her feet on the floor. She tried to stand, then sank back as the ship dropped again. Rebecca reached out to steady herself against the wall.

"I have never been this sick," Mama muttered. "I can't stand." Joseph was rolling back and forth on his bed, his face contorted. The basin slid away from him, and Rebecca bent to set it back on the corner of his cot. Straightening up, she looked at Mama's too-white face.

"Do you want me to get you a damp cloth to lay on your eyes?"

Mama shook her head. "Go see if any of the mates are in their bunks." Rebecca nodded. Mama lifted herself up on one elbow. "If one of the mates can't go find Mr. Pratt, you just come straight back in here."

"I will," Rebecca said.

Mama sank onto her pillow, closing her eyes again. Rebecca turned toward the forward door. She took each step carefully, her hands held out for balance. The storm wasn't getting better. If anything, it was getting worse.

Rebecca lurched through the forward door, using the door handle to steady herself. The mizzenmast was creaking with the force of the wind above. In the lantern light, Rebecca noticed that it looked shiny.

Holding on to the edge of the big table, she reached out and touched the trickle of cold water. It was either raining or the seas were splashing across the deck. Rebecca shivered, bracing herself against the constant motion.

Rebecca was startled by a sudden meowing accompanied by a quick brush of soft, warm fur against her ankle. She reached down to pick up Major. He rubbed his whiskered cheek against her arm, and she looked into his face, leaning most of her weight against the table to keep from stumbling across the room when the ship's bow rose again, tilting the floor.

"What are you doing up here?" she asked Major.

The big black-and-white cat blinked placidly and began to purr.

"You just wait here while I see if any of the mates are close," Rebecca said, shaking her finger in Major's face. He reached up with both front paws and trapped it, biting her gently.

Rebecca laughed and held Major tightly for a second. She envied him. He never got sick when the ship was in heavy seas. Nothing about ship life seemed to bother him at all. If he ever felt cooped up or crowded, it didn't show. Rebecca set Major onto the floor and walked forward.

This door was stuck; the wood was damp and swollen. Rebecca set her feet and pulled harder, almost losing her balance. She clung to the handle and waited until the ship leveled out again. Then she straightened and heaved at the door. It still wouldn't open.

The ship rose, then sank, the stern higher than the bow for a few seconds, then reversing. Worried that she wouldn't be able to get to the mates' cabins, Rebecca stood still, breathing hard. The only other way out would be to use the sternmost door that led up out of the after-cabin. But Mama would never let her go abovedecks in weather like this. Papa had warned them many times that whalers were all too often washed overboard in high seas. The idea of falling into the cold, endless water terrified her.

Rebecca jerked at the handle, and the door suddenly flew open. She took a step backward to catch herself, but the changing angle of the deck made it impossible.

Sitting down hard, Rebecca looked up just as the hatch door opened and someone began to clump down the stairs. In that instant, Major shot past her, darting up the steps.

"Close the hatch!" Rebecca shouted. But it was too late. Mr. Potter, the soft-spoken fourth mate, was already at the base of the stairs, shaking water from his cap by beating it against his leg. He looked up and saw her.

"Mama needs someone to go get an emetic from Mr. Pratt," Rebecca blurted.

"I'm sorry, Miss Whittier," Mr. Potter rasped, turning into his cabin. "I have no time to look for Mr. Pratt now." He talked unevenly, his breathing like a man who had run a long distance. He glanced back at her over his shoulder as he opened his trunk. "We need another compass. Captain Whittier lost hold of his."

Rebecca heard a long roll of thunder as he hurried past her without another word, clomping up the steps so fast that the banging of the hatch startled Rebecca into blinking. Then she began to cry.

CHAPTER EIGHT

John sat in a corner of the forecastle, hunched over near the bunks, his back against the creaking forward mast. The storm was pretty bad, and most of the first watch had come back down belowdecks. Some of the men were sharing bunks. Others had made makeshift pallets on the floor.

John could feel the mast vibrating with the force of the gale outside. He blinked in the lantern light, wishing Russell hadn't gotten hurt. The big man lay in a daze of pain and fever, unable to brace himself against the motion of the ship. It was awful. He kept screaming when his arm was pressed up against the side of the bunk.

John lowered his chin onto his knees, closing his eyes for a few seconds. His stomach was queasy, but not too bad yet. He was glad he hadn't eaten as many doughnuts as he had wanted. Antonio was groaning on his bunk, praying beneath his breath, and John had the uncharitable thought that it served him right.

The hatch overhead slammed open, and John felt a fine spray of seawater spatter his face. A second later, a gush of cool air hit him, and he drew in a deep breath. It was the first mate, Mr. Adams, who came clomping down the steep steps, brushing water from his coat. "A bad evening, John."

"Aye, sir." John stood up.

"Your stomach hold up through all this?" Mr. Adams asked.

John nodded. It was almost true. He rarely got badly seasick. "Mr. Greene is bad off, sir."

Mr. Adams turned to look just as the ship nosed downward dizzyingly. Russell flopped to one side of his bunk and moaned between his teeth. The man above him, Mr. Forbes, cried out. Boston George was up with the few men

Captain Whittier had kept abovedecks. Wherever he was, John was sure he was praying.

Mr. Adams stood with his feet wide, leaning to compensate for the changing slate of the floor. "I came down to find a man who can keep his equilibrium in this kind of weather, John."

John nodded slowly. "I sometimes get a little sick to my stomach, sir. Never dizzy."

"You will do, then," Mr. Adams said, turning on his heel.

John followed him up the dark stairs, wishing he was back home, sitting out this storm in a warm, dry room with a fireplace at one end. As always, when he thought about home and his mother, he felt his eyes sting.

Mr. Adams put his shoulder to the hatch and shoved upward. It yielded slowly, then slammed wide open as the wind caught it. "You're needed up on the mainsail," Mr. Adams shouted above the whistling of the wind in the rigging. Lightning split the sky, and John felt cold rain on his face.

"Aye, sir," John shouted.

"Step lively," Mr. Adams warned, then he strode off toward the helm.

John stared after him, pulling his jacket closer, fastening the button at the top. The wind was fierce, and rain mixed with sea spray pelted the deck. John fought the urge to go back belowdecks and hide. He did not want to be up here.

John closed the hatch with shaking hands. It was partly the sudden onslaught of the storm, but he knew it was his fear, too. He straightened up and thought about his mother again. She walked with her spine straight, her chin high, even when she had no basket on her head. He could not remember even seeing her afraid.

He forced himself to take the first step. The second one was easier, and by the time he had made his way around the tryworks, slipping a little in the grease that remained after the hasty scrub-down, he felt steadier. Lightning blazed again, and the rain fell harder.

The main mast loomed against the sky, disappearing into the darkness. John positioned himself by the copper water tank and looked upward, blinking. He could just see two men straddling the yard.

"Mr. Adams sent me," he called out as loudly as he could.

One of the men leaned down, cupping his hands around his mouth. John recognized Mr. Garner. "Climb up, then, lad. We need another pair of hands."

John staggered forward as the ship's bow lowered, sliding into a trough between swells. He managed to steady himself on the wet rigging, the cold rope grating against his calloused hands.

"Step careful," Mr. Garner yelled.

"Aye, Mr. Garner," John shouted over the racketing of the wind through the rigging. He started up the rope-ladder, his wet jacket flattened against his skin. The wound cloth that covered his head caught the wind and slid up on his forehead, but he managed to keep it on by clapping one hand on top of his head. He paused and pulled it off, sliding it inside his coat pocket. The wind suddenly buffeted John, very nearly knocking him loose from his perch before he could get both hands back on the rope.

A flash of lightning lit the deck below, and John saw Captain Whittier at the wheel, flanked by dark figures with upturned collars and caps pulled low. The captain rarely trusted even Mr. Adams to relieve him when the weather was poor.

Squinting into the wind, John neared the bottom of the horizontal yard and paused, looking up. He was used to crawling on the rope-work rigging and, normally, it didn't bother him at all—not even when he was ordered to climb all the way up to the highest crow's nest. But it was very different tonight. The darkness made it impossible to see much of the deck below, and the noise of the wind blanketed every other sound. Even the familiar creaking of the mast was lost in the high-pitched screech of the gale.

John worked his way upward, until he was high enough to swing one leg out over the yard. He sat, straddling it, looking at Mr. Garner's vague shape in the darkness. Coming from the opposite side, way out on the yardarm, John heard fragments of windblown prayer. It was too dark to see Boston George, but there was no mistaking him, even before the next bolt of lightning illuminated his rain-spattered face.

Mr. Garner waited until John was braced as well as he could be. Then he leaned close. "The halyard broke clean in half as we were lowering the mainsail. The wind tore the canvas some. We can repair it later, but for now we need to get it furled."

John nodded to show that he understood. They had tried to do a three-man job with only two, and the middle of the huge roll of canvas was loose and sagging. In weather like this, the wind would shred loose cloth into rags.

With Mr. Garner calling out orders, they started over, rehoisting the sail to half-mast. The canvas writhed and fluttered like a giant bird fighting for its life. Twice John almost lost his balance trying to control it. Finally, all three of them had their sections of the sail bundled closely against the swaying yard.

"Tie her off, then," Mr. Garner yelled. The

sound of the wind was like a thousand souls shrieking in terror or pain. It carried salt water spray, throwing it against them so hard that it stung like flung pebbles.

The ship struggled against the waves. John was grateful that between the flashes of lightning, he couldn't see them looming close to the *Vigilance*. The sea was huge. The waves looked like a range of hills above the ship. John tightened the last of the knots, running his hands across the soaked canvas.

"Is this the worst storm you've ever seen?" John shouted to Mr. Garner.

There was a bitter laugh. "It's not a storm, John, it's a hurricane!"

John pulled in a deep breath. A hurricane. He had heard the older men tell tales of crewmen washed overboard, whole ships disappearing without a trace.

"All secure?" Mr. Adams shouted from below, jolting John out of his dark thoughts.

"Aye sir," Mr. Garner answered.

"Get yourselves down, then," Mr. Adams yelled up at them.

As John slid down the rigging, Mr. Garner slapped him on the back. "See if you can get some sleep, son. There's not much for anyone to do but recite their prayers now."

Boston George inclined his head to show that he had caught the joke. But he did not stop praying, and John was grateful. For all he knew, it was George's prayers that kept them afloat.

Rebecca started up the steep steps, following the wet boot prints left on the polished floor by Mr. Potter. The hatch was heavy, and she had to use most of her strength to lift the water-laden wood even halfway. Straining to hold the hatch door up far enough so that she could see, Rebecca peered into the howling darkness. She waited for lightning, but the blue-white flash lit monstrous waves that frightened her into letting the weight of the hatch back down.

She turned to sit on the top step, sobbing into her hands. Joseph needed medicine. Rebecca longed for Major's warm, comforting presence. Most likely he had gone down the main companionway. He knew every passage and nook on the ship.

She got to her feet, gathering her skirts, looking at the door that led to the stateroom where her mother and brother lay, so seasick that neither could so much as stand up. The motion of the ship had closed it, but not tightly. She could hear the latch clicking every time the ship rocked forward.

Rebecca clenched her fists and wiped her eyes. Mr. Potter should have gotten Joseph's medicine. She felt her eyes flood with tears again. She heard a roll of thunder as she had to grab at the Scotchman's table. She swayed, her fingers tight on the rail. As the ship rose and fell, inclining the floor again, she took a careful step back toward the stateroom, wondering what in the world she was going to tell her mother. And, she reminded herself, what she was going to say to poor Joseph.

It was the sound of Joseph's painful retching that made her stop, furious with Mr. Potter and with herself. Joseph needed medicine. Rebecca hesitated, gathering her courage. Surely Papa would not get angry with her for trying to help her brother. Nor would Mama. Rebecca turned around and made her way back to the foot of the steep steps, pulling her bonnet from her pocket and tying the strings tightly beneath her chin. She wanted to go back for her jacket, but knew that if she did, Mama would forbid her to go abovedecks.

Struggling against the motion of the ship, she raised the hatch. She could hear shouting, but she could not recognize any of the voices. Rebecca found herself shivering with cold and fear as she lifted the hatch high enough to slide it open.

Rebecca crawled out, staying low as the wind whipped at her skirts. Rain and sea spray spattered her face as the deck slanted and she fell sideways, grabbing the edge of the hatch. She dragged it toward herself, angling the edge to slide it back into place.

It was hard to stand up. The wind was like nothing she had ever felt before, like strong hands clawing at her, shoving her. She crept forward, terrified and shaking as lightning crackled above her, giving everything a sickly, bluish tint. She could hear the rigging whistling in the gale above her head and wondered if the yards and sails could stand the beating they were getting. Just as she reached the main mast, the wind seemed to drop for an instant, then came smashing back, making her lie flat, her arms covering her head.

For a horrible moment, Rebecca could not move. The wind rushed over her in the dark, screaming and howling through the rigging ropes. She cowered, afraid to go forward or backward, her courage failing. She had been foolish to come abovedecks. Desperate, she lifted her chin, squinting, and spotted the patch of dark shadows that filled the entry to the companionway.

Fighting an instinct to turn back, forcing herself to think about Joseph and Mama, she began to inch forward. Her skirts wet and greasy from the unwashed decks, she crawled slowly toward the companionway.

When her fingers finally found the edge of the opening, Rebecca cried out in relief. She pulled herself inside the little three-sided shelter, skidding down the first two steps headfirst, then managing to get turned around. She sat in the darkness, the still air comforting against her skin. Then, gulping down deep breaths, she stood up and continued downward. Behind her, the sky lit in a long, crackling display of lightning. Rebecca shivered. She had never, ever seen a storm as bad as this one.

CHAPTER NINE

Rebecca felt her way along, her right hand extended so that she could catch herself when the ship shifted. She had been in the forward cabin only once in the four years they had been at sea. But she knew that the steep steps led belowdecks, then on down another flight into the hold.

There was a storeroom on this end. Ten times a day she had seen crewmen go down the companionway to find rope or some other sundry supply that was needed. And she knew that the storeroom led into a narrow passage that led past the steward's cabin. The galley was just forward from that.

Rebecca shivered as she came to the bottom

of the companionway. Papa would be furious if he knew she was here now. Joseph had described it to her. From the storeroom up to the forecastle where their bunks were, the men spent their free time down here if the weather was bad. They sat smoking their long-stemmed pipes made out of albatross leg bones, or played mumblety-peg, or worked on their scrimshaw. But they would all be sleeping now, she told herself, or just lying in their bunks or on the floor. Papa insisted on quiet after nine o'clock.

Even without being able to see anything, Rebecca knew that the forward cabin was not as clean as the aft cabin her mother kept. The air was stale and laden with smells. The galley's odors of sour pork and damp biscuits were nearly hidden by the stench of wet hempen rope. She couldn't see the coils stacked against the walls, but she knew they were there. There were piles of canvas, too—spare sails and remnants used for patching. Joseph had found Major hunting for mice down here many times.

Rebecca closed her eyes, hoping desperately that Major had found shelter down here. She couldn't stand the idea of all the bleak months between here and home without him.

The deck shifted and made Rebecca stumble sideways, spinning around in the dark before she fell. The rough wood grated at her cheeks and hands as she hit the deck, and for a moment she lay still, stunned. Then she sat up and gathered her skirts to try to stand again. It was almost impossible, and she sat down hard twice before she managed it.

Once on her feet, she swayed as the ship tilted. Then, her arms extended in a futile attempt to regain her balance, she reeled sideways. When she straightened up again, she realized she had no idea which direction to go. Fighting to keep upright, she turned in an awkward, stiff-legged circle. There was no light in any direction.

The darkness seemed to close in around Rebecca, and she found herself pulling in quick, shallow breaths as she tried to figure out what to do. The creaking of the timbers and the planking gave her no clues.

Wobbling, Rebecca set off. Any direction was better than standing still. She kept her steps short and stopped every time the ship's movement threatened her balance. She hummed to herself at first, then began to whisper in the black lightless hold.

"I will come to the doorway eventually," she assured herself. "I will find a wall and follow it around." Her whisper was lost in the muted shrieking of the wind—loud even down here. But the simple act of talking aloud seemed to give her courage. "Just keep going," she instructed herself, placing one foot, then the other on the heaving planks.

A sharp jolting of the deck made her hesitate midstep. She thrust her hands out, striking her wrist on something cold and hard an instant before she stumbled against it. Instinctively scrabbling for a handhold, she found herself gripping the edge of a bin. Holding herself still against it, she heard metal sliding. The next wrenching jolt of the ship threw her forward, and she pitched headfirst into the bin, her hands sliding over a jumble of metal and wood as she caught herself.

As the ship eased into momentary steadiness, she pushed herself backward, recognizing the wedge-shaped blade of an ax beneath her right hand. On her feet, Rebecca stood trembling in the darkness.

The storm was getting worse, she was sure of it. The ship was tilting more steeply all the time. The waves must be huge. And she could sometimes hear the slow roll of thunder above the creaking of the ship. Gathering her courage again, Rebecca forced herself to feel her way past the tool bin. It was hard to make herself let go of it, but she finally took one step away, then another.

As she fought her way along, she thought about Joseph, wretchedly sick, and Mama, no better off. Rebecca frowned. She had done nothing to help anyone, and was only going to be a worry for Papa if he found a few seconds to go belowdecks to see Mama.

Longing for a lantern, wishing that she had

thought to bring even a candle to use down here, Rebecca set off again. She stumbled into barrels and tripped over coils of rope before her searching fingers found the solid planking of a wall. But once she had, she could move twice as fast, even though she sometimes had to make her way around stacks of supplies.

When Rebecca finally did come to a gap in the wall, she exhaled in relief. The sound of a meow brought her swinging around. "Major?" she whispered, then cleared her throat. "Major!"

As she sank to the deck, careful to keep her back against the guiding wall, she felt a soft brush of warm fur against her cheek. A second later, Major's familiar thrumming purr told her he was as glad to find her as she was to have found him.

The wind had gotten worse in the short time John had been aloft. He had followed Mr. Garner back to the forward hatch through a pelting rain. They had both walked like hunched old men, planting each foot heavily and carefully. Mr. Garner kept a path that never took them more than a half-step away from rope and rigging. He made his way from one handhold to the next, and John imitated him almost exactly as the flashes of lightning lit the heavens above them.

Together they pulled the forward hatch cover to one side. John went down first and stood waiting at the bottom of the steps. Mr. Garner struggled to replace the hatch, and John started back up the narrow stairs to help, then stopped when he realized there was no way the two of them could stand side by side.

Mr. Garner finally got the hatch secure, and John led the way down into the forecastle. It felt odd to be in still air after having been out so long in the wind. As they pulled dry clothes from their trunks, Mr. Garner began to talk. "We'll be lucky to keep from turning turtle tonight."

John pulled on his dry spare shirt and stared at the older man. "You think the *Vigilance* could go over?" John bent to pull off his soaked trousers and reached for his dry pants.

Mr. Garner shook his head, laying his own wet clothing over the top of his trunk. "Don't listen to me, son. I just don't like hurricanes."

"No one likes them," a voice came out of the darkness.

John shook out his coat, then put it back on. The only lantern was in a wire rack on the far wall, and deep shadows hid the speaker, but he knew Mr. Jackson's voice.

"It wouldn't be so bad if Russell Greene would stop moaning. I can't hardly sleep knowing he's so bad off."

Mr. Garner nodded. "If there is laudanum in the medicine store, someone should dose him for the night at least."

"It's only decent," Mr. Jackson answered. "This weather is hard on a healthy man."

John looked at Mr. Garner. "Laudanum? What's that?"

"It's what the high and mighty take so that they never have to feel a toothache," Mr. Jackson said from his dark bunk.

"It would stop Russell's pain?" John shook his head, unable to believe such a thing. The only cure he had ever heard of for pain was whiskey—and that often seemed to leave men feeling worse off once they got sober.

"I have to stand morning watch," Mr. Garner said. "I take Russell's place." He sounded apologetic, but he crossed the room, and John could hear him climbing into his bunk.

Russell groaned as a particularly bad roll of the ship rocked him onto his wounded arm. John winced, imagining how it must feel. Russell's eyes were wide open but they looked dull, and he didn't seem to notice John standing so close by.

"Mr. Pratt is probably in his bunk by now," Mr. Jackson said. "I guess it'll have to wait until morning."

John glanced at the bunks. Half the men were lying awake, their eyes wide open. If Mr. Pratt wasn't sleeping, he might not mind getting the laudanum for Russell. John nodded vaguely in the direction of Mr. Garner's bunk, then turned, his thoughts spinning.

Getting medicine for Russell was the right thing to do, and John knew it. But as thunder clashed so loudly he would have sworn the deck shook beneath his feet, he wondered if anything anyone did made a difference now. This was a hurricane. They could all be dead before morning.

CHAPTER TEN

Every step was hard. The wind had turned savage, and John could no longer push away images of the endless water that roared and rushed against the planks of the ship's hull. But even though he had heard a hundred stories about hurricanes, he knew not every ship sank. Some made it through. Still, the idea that only a few boards separated him from sure death made him shiver, then dig his fingernails into his palms.

At the rear of the forecastle, the door into the cooper's workshop was already wide open, the low flicker of a tin oil lamp casting dancing amber shapes upon the wall. John passed through as quietly as he could, struggling not to fall into the piles of staves and rims that were sliding to one side, then back again.

Mr. Nilsen was snoring in the little cabin off to the starboard side of his workshop, and John was glad. He was a touchy man, often angry at anyone who trespassed into his part of the ship except to pass through on their way to the galley. He carried a long knife, and there were rumors about how many fights it had won him.

John could barely make his way forward, and he envied Mr. Jackson and all the others in their bunks. He wanted nothing more than to be in his own bed now, dozing and praying and, with God's help, waking up in the morning to find the hurricane had passed. Sleeping anywhere sounded like heaven on Earth. No one had offered *him* a bunk, or even a spare blanket. He wondered if any of the others would have given over their beds to an injured man. A few might, he decided. Most of them wouldn't.

A sudden jolting of the ship made John crash to his knees. As he scrambled back to his feet, the clattering of metal barrel rims on the far side of the room drowned out all other sound for a few seconds. The ship righted itself. John kept his feet, walking in a half-crouch, eyeing the smoky oil lamp in its wall sconce. If the weather got much heavier, it should be put out.

John braced himself for a few seconds in the doorway at the far end of the cooper's workshop. Then he pushed off again, feeling his way through the darkness of the narrow corridor that ran through the storeroom and pantry. He could smell the pervasive, cloying odor of salt pork, and it made his stomach clench.

Somewhere, in the locked pantries on the port side, there was a dull thudding sound, then the grind of metal against metal. The casks of meat and oil—as well as the barrels of flour—were all enormously heavy. If the storm tipped many onto their sides and they began rolling with the motion of the ship, it'd be dangerous to be down here. It'd be even worse in the hold, where the heavy barrels of oil would be shifting back and forth.

The galley was dark, too, but quieter. The tables and benches were all fastened down and helped John steady himself as he walked. The timbers overhead creaked with the motion of the ship, and it was still hard to keep his balance, but John felt himself calming down a little. The *Vigilance* was a sound-built ship, and Captain Whittier kept it in good repair. He was one of the best helmsmen in New Bedford. They stood a good chance of riding out this hurricane.

Leaning on the edges of the tables, John negotiated the width of the galley faster than he had come through the other rooms. On the far side, he had to feel his way across the wall, searching for the door that led into Mr. Pratt's cabin. When he finally felt the handle, he used it to balance himself while he freed one hand to knock.

"Who's there?" came a shout.

"John Lowe, sir!"

There was a long silence after that, long enough to make John wonder if Mr. Pratt had simply gone back to sleep. Then, abruptly, the door opened inward, and John stumbled through the lighted doorway.

"Easy there, lad," Mr. Pratt growled.

John fought for his balance, trying not to

blunder into any of the steward's furniture. A bed and a narrow writing desk flanked the walls. A huge sea trunk stood below the footboard. John noticed a stack of account books in a closed shelf that hung from the wall. The lantern—a tall, glass chimney shielding the wick—was in a sconce that held it securely in place against the tilting wall. The candle was not smoking. Mr. Pratt must have just trimmed the wick.

"What brings you?" Mr. Pratt demanded.

John felt himself getting angry. "It's Mr. Greene, sir. He's in a bad way."

"I know that," Mr. Pratt snapped. "If that's all you have come to tell me—"

"No, sir," John interrupted. "Mr Garner said—"

"Mr. Garner's opinions are hardly my concern," Mr. Pratt interrupted. Raising one hand to his mouth, he swallowed heavily and John realized that he was seasick. That meant he would be even shorter-tempered than usual. He was glowering now, as though he expected John to say something.

"Excuse me sir, I—"

"What brings you, boy?" Mr. Pratt exploded.

"Laudanum," John managed. "Mr. Greene needs laudanum."

A sudden lurch of the ship sent them stumbling aft. Mr. Pratt sat awkwardly on the edge of his bed as John grabbed at the footboard, struggling to keep himself from sprawling on the steward's blankets.

Mr. Pratt lowered his head, his hands over his eyes, and John knew he was fighting nausea. When he looked up, his mouth was a tight, thin line. "Laudanum is expensive," he said sharply, as though John had claimed differently.

"But Russell is in a lot of pain, sir," John persisted. "He's in my bunk and—"

"Laudanum is not going to cure him," Mr. Pratt said coldly. "If you need a place to sleep, you should talk to Captain Whittier."

John fought to keep from losing his temper at the insult. "Russell is my friend," he said, measuring every word. "If laudanum would ease him, he should have it."

Mr. Pratt met John's eyes for the first time,

and John forced himself to keep his gaze steady even as the floor tipped steeply again. He had to grab the footboard once more to keep from pitching forward.

"All right, then," Mr. Pratt gave in. "Do you have a bottle to put it in?"

John shook his head. "No, sir."

Mr. Pratt's face was a mask of exasperation, but he stood and opened the massive sea chest. One hand on the footboard to hold himself upright, he bent and reached in. A few seconds later, he had a small bottle in his right hand and a glass flask in the other. John eyed the brown-ish liquid as Mr. Pratt waited for a second's lull in the ship's pitching motion.

When it came, he poured a spoonful of the medicine into the empty bottle, then quickly replaced both corks.

"There," Mr. Pratt said, thrusting the bottle at John. "He can thank the storm that I slipped and poured enough for morning, too."

John held the little bottle up to the lantern, leaning on the doorjamb to steady himself. It was such a tiny amount. It was hard to believe that it could do anything to help anyone.

The sound of the cat meowing made John turn around, keeping one hand on the door frame for balance.

"John Lowe? Is that you?"

John peered into the darkness. "Miss Whittier?"

The captain's daughter stepped closer, and the dim light from Mr. Pratt's lantern revealed her. She was soaking wet, and her dress was dirty. In her arms, she held her bedraggled cat.

"Miss Whittier?" Mr. Pratt demanded, looking over John's shoulder. "Whatever are you doing down here?"

"My mother needs an emetic for Joseph. He's terribly sick."

John stepped aside and stood, swaying with the motion of the ship. Miss Whittier's teeth were chattering. The cat wriggled in her arms, and she clutched it closer.

"This is a hurricane, Miss Whittier," Mr. Pratt said sternly. "You should be with your family."

John saw her eyes go wide and knew that she had heard as many stories as he had about hurricanes. But she braced herself and kept her head. "Do you have an emetic?" she asked again after a second's pause.

Mr. Pratt glanced back toward his open trunk. "An emetic sometimes helps an adult. It is a harsh cure for a child his size," he said.

"Mama said an emetic helped once," Miss Whittier argued.

Mr. Pratt shrugged and made his way back to the trunk. As he bent to reach down inside, John glanced again at Miss Whittier. She looked exhausted.

The ship rolled, and John staggered a half-step to his right, nearly bumping into Miss Whittier. He apologized, and she smiled at him. "It's hardly your fault."

Mr. Pratt turned, a phial of yellowish liquid in his hand. "Tell your mother I said to give Joseph half of this now and the rest when he wakens in the morning. I have no more, so tell her not to waste a drop."

Miss Whittier nodded solemnly as she took the bottle and tucked it into her sash. "I will, sir. And thank you."

Mr. Pratt caught John's eye. "Get her back safe with her mother before you take that laudanum to Mr. Greene."

John was reluctant, and it must have shown on his face.

"That's an order, boy."

"Yes, sir," John answered.

"Use this." Mr. Pratt lit a candle stub and set it into a small box lantern. "She has no business being down here," he said as he handed it to John, speaking as though Miss Whittier were deaf.

A second later, the steward stepped back inside his room and shut the door hard. John could hear a latch being lowered into place. He looked at Miss Whittier. "Are you ready, Miss?"

She shook her head. "Take the laudanum to Mr. Greene first. Major and I will wait for you here."

John lifted the lantern to get a better look at her face. "I can't leave you alone. Your father—"

"I saw Mr. Greene's arm," Miss Whittier said deliberately. "He must be in terrible pain."

John nodded. "He is."

Miss Whittier hesitated, then gestured. "Go, then. Just please hurry back."

"Keep this." John held out the lantern. She hooked one arm under the cat, freeing a hand to take it just as the ship shifted hard to one side. They both staggered backward. Without thinking, John grabbed her wrist to keep her from falling and breaking the lantern. When she had her footing, he released her arm and lowered his eyes.

She nodded. "Thank you."

John shrugged, feeling awkward. He wasn't used to talking to girls, especially wealthy girls like Miss Whittier. If she told her father that he had touched her, it would cause trouble, he knew. He took a step back.

Miss Whittier lifted the lantern to look around. "I'll be right over there." She jutted out her chin to gesture toward the far wall where piles of canvas were stacked by the galley door.

John nodded. Her father would hang him by his thumbs if anything happened to her, but he couldn't stand the thought of Russell lying groaning and sweating any longer.

Against his better judgment, glancing back to make sure that Miss Whittier was settled against the wall now, John started forward.

CHAPTER ELEVEN

Rebecca sat on the pile of sail canvas. The ship was rolling as hard as she had ever felt it, and it scared her. The thunder seemed to start beneath the ship, not above, a strange, penetrating rumble. The little lantern braced between her ankles, she sat scratching Major's ears as the sound of the wind wailed above. She could hear the masts creaking, long, painful sounds that made it seem as though the wood were being tortured.

So this was a hurricane. Rebecca thought about her father, up on deck, struggling to hold the wheel steady. How could he even stand up against the force of the wind? Would there be a time when he would have to give up and come back into the after-cabin and pray with Mama? If that happened, Rebecca wanted to be there with her family.

Major wriggled out of her grasp, and she reached to pull him back, sliding her feet away from the lantern. It stood steadily enough, but she kept an eye on it as she bent to press her cheek against Major's warm fur.

"No, stay close," she pleaded with him. He turned in a small circle, his tail a flag as he arched his back for her to scratch. He seemed so calm, so normal, that Rebecca felt the sharp edge of her fear dull a little.

"You frightened me, running out the door like that," Rebecca scolded him. He meowed.

She reached out to slide the lantern closer, then lifted Major to stare into his eyes. "I will have to tell Elizabeth and Hope that we came through a hurricane together," she said, and tried to smile.

Just then, the *Vigilance* rolled hard to starboard, and Rebecca held her breath. The pitching scared her, but this scared her more. A ship that rolled far enough sideways stood at risk of taking on water and sinking.

One hand on the lantern, Rebecca held Major tightly, her heart thudding. The ship wasn't righting itself. The wall she sat beside slowly became a slanted floor as the deck shifted. She slid sideward, extending one foot to brace herself. There were shouts coming from the forecastle.

The ship stayed over for what seemed like an eternity. Rebecca managed to hold on to the lantern as the ship slowly righted itself. Breathing hard, she clutched at Major, even though he clawed at her sleeve, trying to free himself. As the ship leveled out, the cat calmed down—but Rebecca's mind was swirling as she set the lantern down again.

What if the ship had gone all the way over? Why was she just sitting here alone, waiting for John to come back and escort her across all of twenty feet of open deck? She remembered the wind, the hammering strength of it, but it scared her less than dying alone. She picked up the lantern and got to her feet. Then she began to walk, swaying as she staggered forward.

★   ★   ★

John tipped the bottle against Russell's lips, fighting to hold it steady in spite of the continuous pitching of the ship.

"Thank you," Russell managed.

John nodded. He handed Russell the bottle and watched as the big man checked the stopper, then slid it into his shirtfront. "Remember what I told you," John said.

Russell nodded, closing his eyes. "I'll save the rest until morning."

"I hope it works," John said.

Russell didn't open his eyes, or answer, and John took another step backward. He waited a few seconds, shifting his weight from one foot to the other. Then he turned and started back toward the storeroom, where Miss Whittier was waiting for him.

The cooper's lantern was still lit, and John walked as fast as he could, hesitating when he had to in order to keep his balance. He looked at the smoky wick again as he went past and wondered if he should blow it out. What would Captain Whittier do if he saw it untended like this, with Nilsen in his cabin?

The ship heeled to the starboard, and John paused beside the lantern, close enough to watch the level of the whale oil in the glass reservoir change, slanting. He stood, his heart racing, as the angle deepened. Somewhere in the shadows on the other side of the cooper's workshop, a barrel fell over and rolled.

John heard some of the men curse, then the sound of Boston George's prayers. He added his own as the ship listed and he could not help but imagine the weight of the rigging, the huge masts. If a certain point of balance was passed, the ship would founder.

At what seemed like an impossible pitch, the whole ship shuddered, then she slowly rose again, righting herself. John found himself grinning and he heard a cheer go up in the forecastle. He glanced at Mr. Nilsen's door and expected to see the volatile cooper emerge at any second, but he didn't.

John went onward with trembling legs. If they sank, the only chance of surviving would be to get the three boats launched before the

Vigilance went down. Would they be able to do that with almost all hands belowdecks?

John struggled on, pausing at the door that led into the storeroom. Both arms extended for balance, he kept going. The galley's bolted tables and benches gave him ready handholds, and he made it past them quickly.

As the ship was pounded by the hurricane, its timbers straining, John stared into the darkness, expecting at any second to see the light from Miss Whittier's lantern. He was startled when he reached the galley door and peered through—the storeroom was dark.

"Miss Whittier?"

John waited for an answer, but none came. Through the hull of the ship he heard a thunderclap, then a deep, resonant roar as it faded. He took a step inside the storeroom, cleared his throat, and pitched his voice louder. Still no response.

John stood unsteadily, wondering what he should do next. If her father had come to get her, or even one of the mates, it might be foolish to go chasing after them, as much as admitting that he hadn't followed Mr. Pratt's order. But at the same time, what if she had decided to go alone? What if the wind lifted her overboard? She was small-boned and frail and she would be hanging on to her cat. It could happen all too easily.

John started walking again, veering to one side so that he wouldn't have to pass Mr. Pratt's door too closely. The last thing he wanted was to have to explain.

John made his way through the dark store-room at the far end of the forward cabin. It wasn't easy—open expanses of deck offered no handholds, nothing to lean upon or brace against. He fell twice and wondered how Miss Whittier could have managed carrying both her cat and the lantern.

Rebecca stopped at the bottom of the companionway, staring up at the darkness, watching the flashes of lightning flicker blue and white. The lantern faltered, then went out. She shuddered, angry at herself. It would have gone out on deck, almost certainly, but she would have had its company for a little longer if she had been careful. She set the lantern down on the bottom step, freeing her hand. She shifted Major from beneath her arm and held him tightly against her chest.

The roaring of the wind was nearly deafening. The sound of it rushing through the rope-rigging was unearthly, terrifying. Major twisted in her arms, and she struggled to hold on to him.

"All we have to do is cross the deck once. And not even all the way. It's just from here to the after-cabin door."

Major meowed, wriggling around to look up into her face.

"We'll be fine," Rebecca told him, knowing that she was trying to convince herself. The roar of the wind was incredible. She placed one foot on the steep stairs, took a deep breath, and started upward, shivering.

The little shed that sheltered the entrance to the companionway was vibrating under the assault of the wind. The ship shook and trembled, and Rebecca lurched sideways, striking her shoulder. Crying, she forced herself to take a step forward, out of the companionway and into the wind. The gale hit her hard and swept her feet from beneath her. Fighting the mad whirling of her skirt with one hand, holding on to Major with the other, she stood up slowly.

Afraid to move, but more afraid to stay still, she took another step, holding on to a coil of rope that hung from the main mast. Trying hard to keep her footing, she took another step, reaching for another handhold. The wind was ferocious, shoving at her. Lightning flashed to the north, a paler flicker of light.

Major meowed and squirmed, his tail lashing as Rebecca kept going. She walked crabwise on the slippery deck, turning her head away from the painfully fierce wind that whipped her hair across her face. Major was wiggling, trying hard to get free. Using both hands to hold on to him, Rebecca lost her balance once more and fell. Major leaped from her arms as the bottle of medicine dropped from her sash and skidded across the slanting deck. Rebecca grabbed at it and missed.

"Major!"

Fighting to regain her feet, Rebecca saw him slide on the wet planks, tumbled by the wind. He sprang up, yowling, and skirted the companionway opening. Frantic, Rebecca lunged, bending to scoop Major up into her arms, but he ricocheted off her ankle, spitting and hissing. Without stopping, his hindquarters churning, he kept going, disappearing into the darkness that hid the bow of the ship.

Rebecca stood, stunned by the suddenness of what had happened. She faced the after-cabin, trying to see the bottle of medicine, but it was gone. The wind shoved her forward two steps before she could turn back toward the bow. If Major could not get belowdecks, he would probably not survive the storm. She began to cry harder, the wind beating at her back.

Torn, her thoughts spinning from her own fear to the danger Major was in, then back to her mother and Joseph, Rebecca stood hunched against the violent wind. Then she started after Major, walking slowly, hanging on to the mast ropes again, then the harpoon lockers.

It was drier now that the lightning storm was passing, but the wind had become a fury, tearing at her clothes. Every step required all of her courage. The deck was tipping and jarring beneath her feet, and she clung to the edge of the knee-high brick wall that surrounded the tryworks.

Afraid to go any farther, Rebecca stopped just short of the forward hatch and peered into the dark, trying to catch a glimpse of Major. She could not. Chilled through and scared, she started to turn back, then noticed a flash of white in the rigging that hung from the foremast.

"Major!" she shouted, wiping at her tears. But the sound of her voice was drowned out by the screaming wind.

She worked her way to the base of the rigging, then held on to the ropes, looking upward. Distant lightning sparked. Major had not gone very high, but he was out of reach.

Rebecca's hands were shaking as she pulled herself up onto the rigging. As she climbed, she could see Major's white-and-black face, his eyes squeezed shut against the wind. But as she reached for him, the wind lifted her, swinging the rigging in a wide circle. Rebecca screamed. Startled, Major jumped away from her, clawing his way upward.

CHAPTER TWELVE

John nearly kicked over the lantern Miss Whittier had left on the bottom step. He picked it up, then felt his way down the wall to hang it from a lantern hook. Making his way back, he hesitated only for an instant. Even if she was safely back with her family, he had to look for her.

The companionway steps seemed steeper than usual because the ship slanted in a long roll as he began to climb. Just as he stepped out into the wind the ship leveled again, and he nearly fell, stopping himself from falling back down the steps by clutching at the door frame. The rain was lighter now, but the whipping wind chilled him instantly.

John regained his footing, hesitating, unsure what to do. The fierce wind lulled. In the sudden pause, above the hissing thunder of the sea, he heard a faint but unmistakable scream from the bow.

Whirling around, he started off only to be rebuffed by a sudden harsh gust of wind that made him skid backward on the wet and greasy deck. He bent forward, using the wide, spraddle-legged walk that the older crewmen used in rough weather. Inch by inch he managed to propel himself toward the bow.

"Miss Whittier?" he shouted into the wind. The only answer was a louder howling of the storm.

John kept to the center of the ship, afraid of the invisible ocean that convulsed beneath the thin-planked hull of the *Vigilance*. The brick wall of the tryworks steadied him for a few steps, then he braced himself against the water tank. Just past it, he had to straighten up and walk without handholds for a step or two. He felt like a seed in the wind, like the gale would pick him up and toss him into the water at any moment. He squinted, trying to see in the darkness. The lightning was too far away now to be of any help.

"John! John Lowe!"

He couldn't place the direction of her voice in the wind and he turned in a circle, trying to spot her. When she shouted again, he looked upward in disbelief. Miss Whittier had climbed the rigging! He reached out and caught hold of the rope and started upward.

"Get down!" he shouted at her as the wind caught at him, blowing him backward like so much sail canvas. He held on as the rope-ladder arched under the pressure of the wind. He could just make out the circle of Miss Whittier's pale, frightened face in the darkness and barely hear her response.

"Major is up there! He keeps going higher!"

"Come down!" John tried to make his voice carry over the shrieking wind. But as he watched, Miss Whittier placed one foot in the next rung up.

"No!" he screamed. "I'll get the cat! Come down!"

Miss Whittier seemed not to hear him this time. Helpless to stop her, John could only watch as she moved away from him on the loose rope netting. His shirt belled out as the wind found its way beneath it. He shivered as seawater spattered his face and hands.

Steadying himself, John started to climb after Miss Whittier. The wind howled in his ears, and he clung to the wet, stiff rope, telling himself that she would not keep going, that the height, even without wind, would soon scare her into giving up on reaching her cat.

But she did keep going, just a foot or two at a time, stopping every few seconds to try to cajole the terrified animal into coming down. It stayed just out of her reach, drawing her upward. Shouting at her, John followed, angry at her and at himself. She was risking their lives for a cat! John kept climbing, screaming at her to stop, but unwilling to start down without her. He was sure she would soon look downward and realize how high she had gone—the danger she was in.

As he slipped his right foot out of the netting

and reached for a new handhold, John felt a strange shudder go through the ship. It was gone as quickly as he had felt it, and it was impossible for him to know whether or not he had imagined it—until it came again.

Miss Whittier had felt it, too, John knew, the instant he looked back up at her. She had frozen midstep, the wind flattening her dress against her legs, her hair snaking over her shoulders. She had lost her bonnet.

"Come down!" John shouted up at her again. He felt another jolting shudder in the ship.

"What was that?" Miss Whittier cried out.

John could only shake his head. A second later, the sharp shock came again. This time, the ship rolled to the starboard, slanting farther than it ever had. John could not see in the darkness, but he was sure that the top of the mast was leaning way out over the water.

"John!" Miss Whittier shrieked.

He looked at her. The ship had listed so far to the starboard that the rigging was at a severe slant. Miss Whittier was no longer straight above him. As he watched, her right foot skidded off the wet rope.

"Hang on," John shouted at her. Through the constant noise of the wind, he heard a jumble of faint voices from the deck below.

Rebecca's hands were aching with cold and strain when she lost her foothold. The wind slamming against her, she managed to hang on, regaining her footing. Major was somewhere higher in the rigging, and poor John Lowe was in grave danger because of her. Clinging to the rope netting, she heard bits and pieces of shouts borne upward by the wind. Looking down, she realized for the first time that she was so high that the deck was almost invisible in the darkness.

Terrified, she tried to move one foot downward. She toed at the rigging, searching for an opening big enough to provide a foothold—but she couldn't. The slant of the mast had collapsed the heavy rope netting.

As Rebecca struggled not to fall, a small rectangle of amber light below her made her turn toward the stern and stare. For a fleeting second, she saw a silhouette of Mama carrying Joseph in her arms, his feet dangling. Then the figures vanished so suddenly that Rebecca knew their lantern had been extinguished by the wind.

"They're lowering the boats!" John shouted.

There was such terror in his voice that Rebecca felt a cold wave of desperation. That meant Papa believed the ship was going to sink. A few seconds later, piercing the whine of the wind was a high-pitched squeaking—the davit winches were being turned. "Papa!" she screamed. "Papa! I'm up here!" John began to shout, too, and Rebecca could feel the rigging shaking as he twisted and turned, trying to make himself heard.

No one answered and, as far as she could tell, no one could hear them. The continuous clamor of the hurricane winds had obliterated their voices.

Rebecca felt a cold, awful weight settle in her stomach. The *Vigilance* was going to sink, and she and John were trapped. She glanced upward at Major, where he hung in a miserable cat-curve on the ropes, barely visible in the darkness. If she hadn't tried to chase him, Rebecca thought, she would be getting into one of the boats with her family and John would be down with the other crewmen.

Rebecca tried to find a foothold again, kicking at the stiff, soaked hemp, the rough fiber grating at her palms. "Up here!" she screamed. "Papa, look at me!" But it did no good. Staring downward, her eyes narrowed against the stinging gale, Rebecca could just see the scurrying of shadows along the slanted deck. She could not make out who they were, or whether or not they were looking for her and John.

The mast swayed heavily, and Rebecca clutched tighter at the rigging, wedging her left foot into the ropes. She shouted over and over, but the dark figures ran back and forth, then the decks were empty, with all the crew gathered beside the boats. The lowering did not take long. The three little boats rose and fell on the surface of the swells, and their white hulls were like beacons in the dark.

As the wind scattered Rebecca's tears, she

closed her eyes, knowing her father had done his duty by his ship, his men, and his family—in that order. If he thought that she had somehow fallen overboard, he would not spare a single man to come back and look for her—or for John. And what else could he possibly think if he had sent crewmen to look belowdecks and they were nowhere to be found?

CHAPTER THIRTEEN

John's hands were nearly numb. Helpless, he had watched the three overcrowded boats as the men rowed astern, shouting out the count to steady themselves. Then, he had fallen into a kind of stupor, his eyes closed and his mind whirling with thoughts that had no purpose.

As the wind whistled around him, he pondered how oddly little bits of luck added up to life, or to death. If he and Miss Whittier had not climbed this high, the captain would have seen them easily. If the cat hadn't run up the rigging in the first place, Miss Whittier never would have followed. If he had not tried to help her . . .

The mast suddenly swung lower, and John opened his eyes, crying out without meaning to. Miss Whittier screamed. John looked down. He could just make out the tryworks and the deckhouse. But the outline of the ship against the dark water was distinct now. He glanced at the horizon. Dawn was not far off. He scanned the ocean for the white hulls of the boats, but couldn't spot any of them.

The mast dropped another few inches, then bobbed back up. Miss Whittier screamed at the sudden motion. He looked up at her. She hung limply from the ropes, her hair wet and matted across her brow.

"I'm sorry," she called to him after a moment, and he realized that even though the wind was still fierce, it had dropped in force. He could hear her clearly. He took a breath to answer, but the abrupt rise of the mast stopped him.

Amazed, afraid to hope, John felt the rigging straighten a little, the rope netting opening up. He loosed one hand, meaning to climb down-ward, and very nearly fell. He heard Miss Whittier's shout and saw her feet dangling above him. She had lost both her footholds now and was clinging to the ropes with only her hands.

Making fists, trying to squeeze life back into his fingers, John forced his aching knees to bend, his cramped arms to reach upward. Hooking his wrists through the rope webbing, he started toward her. "Don't move," he warned Miss Whittier.

"I didn't mean to, I—" she broke off, and John didn't answer her as he climbed, feeling as slow as a snail, and as thick-witted. When the mast rose again, it took him a full minute to realize that the webbing had opened up completely.

"You can do it," he tried to shout to Miss Whittier, reaching to grab her high-laced shoe. He guided her foot forward, into the webbing. She placed her other foot without help, then looked at him, blinking in surprise. "Is the *Vigilance* righting herself?"

He nodded, unable to speak, praying that it was true.

She turned, reaching, and he saw her pulling Major toward herself. The cat seemed docile now, exhausted. Once it was safely in Miss Whittier's arms, she undid her broad sash, with one hand, then awkwardly retied it, making a sling. The cat seemed content to lie still within the soft cloth.

As John watched, Miss Whittier twisted around, lifting her chin, and he knew she was looking for the boats. He scanned the water, too. The huge swells had fallen. The sea wasn't calm, but the rocking of the ship wasn't alarming now. Still, the boats were nowhere to be seen in the murky gray light. He had been so certain that he and Miss Whittier would die. Were they the only ones who had lived?

As the wind dropped further, the mast rose once more. It was still slanted, but now they were no longer hanging out over the water. John started down, glancing upward to make sure that Miss Whittier was following him.

John climbed slowly, hindered by his cramped and aching muscles. Miss Whittier almost kept pace and stepped onto the deck only a moment after he did. Major slid from beneath her sash, landing on his feet. In a flash of black-and-white fur, he darted forward, running toward the companionway.

John faced into the wind, narrowing his eyes, and stood steadily without bracing himself. It was definitely easing up.

"Look." Miss Whittier was pointing. John saw that the helm had been tied hurriedly, the ropes sprawled across the deck. He walked toward the stern, skirting the deckhouse, then approached the big wooden wheel. It seemed secure enough, and the seas were much calmer now. Was it safe to leave it tied like this? John glanced at Miss Whittier. She looked as uncertain as he did.

"I pray that my family is all right," she said, turning to look out to sea.

John followed her gaze past the slanting masts. The sun was coming up, the eastern horizon flushed rose and blue. He wondered how far the wind had blown the boats and if he would ever see Mr. Jackson or Mr. Garner or his friend Russell again.

John looked toward the after-hatch. Miss Whittier gathered her tangled hair in one hand

and squinted to look into the wind. "What? What are you thinking?"

"Russell Greene," John told her, starting to walk. "He might have gotten left behind." Miss Whittier fell in beside him, matching his stiff stride. They stayed on deck, going the length of the ship to the forward hatch, and John was surprised when she bent to help him slide it open. He gestured, and she led the way down.

He followed, amazed at the quiet—at the stillness of the air. The slanting stairs made the passage feel unfamiliar. There was a little light from the open hatch, but only a little. Ahead of him, Miss Whittier made an odd, soft sound of surprise.

"There's water," she told him. "Ankle deep. It won't come over your boots, I don't think."

He came down the last crooked step slowly. He could hear the gentle sloshing of the water as the ship rolled on the choppy sea. "Russell?" He said it loudly, then listened. There was no sound of labored breathing, no sound at all. John went past Miss Whittier, feeling his way along the bunks. Russell was not here. "They must have taken him," he said aloud, not know-ing whether he should be relieved, or even more worried for his friend.

"Papa thought the ship was going to sink or else he never would have left her," Miss Whittier said. "And if he'd thought that, he never would have left an injured man aboard."

Suddenly, the ship listed farther to starboard. The floor slanted so sharply that John heard the sound of water running across the planks. Then another, louder noise caught John's attention. It was low rumbling, followed by a heavy thud.

"The oil barrels?" John said aloud, and sud-denly he understood. "They've shifted."

Miss Whittier's quick nod told John he didn't need to explain further. "We need a lantern," she said.

He crossed the forecastle, then walked the wall, searching. He found the sconce bracket and was relieved when his fingers brushed against cool glass. Pulling his matches from his pocket, he lit the wick and lowered the glass chimney again. The flickering flame cast his long shadow on the empty bunks.

John gestured again, and Miss Whittier followed, lifting her skirts to wade through the forecastle, then the cooper's workroom. John stopped long enough to take the cooper's lantern off its hook and light it, too. He handed it to Miss Whittier. Together, they made their way forward to the main companionway, then followed the steep steps downward into the hold.

In the amber lantern light, John saw what he had expected. There was some water, but that wasn't what was making the ship list. The oil barrels had shifted to the starboard side and lay in a jumble, some on end, some on their sides. Captain Whittier had to have known, but the storm wouldn't have allowed him to reposition the cargo.

"Do you think we can move them?" Miss Whittier asked, and John turned to look at her.

"Your father would hardly approve of—"

Miss Whittier was nodding. "But we can say you did it all."

He found himself smiling at her as they found niches for their lanterns. His legs, heavy with fatigue and strain, loosened up as they strung ropes across the hold and set to work.

It was hardest at first. With the deck slanting, they had to roll every barrel uphill, using the ropes as temporary holds while they caught their breath.

Midmorning, they stopped to eat, treating themselves from a jar of honey they found in the galley, soaking their hardtack in the sweet, sticky luxury.

By afternoon, the ship had straightened somewhat. They stopped working long enough to eat cold hardtack again, sitting on the deck, too tired to talk.

It was sunny. The wind had dropped to no more than a strong breeze, and John saw a goney flying high above the ship. He found himself constantly sweeping the surface of the ocean with his eyes and noticed Miss Whittier doing the same. If they were truly lost, he wondered how long they could possibly survive.

Rebecca was so tired that she felt dizzy, but when they finally rolled the last barrel to port and stood back, swaying on their feet, she felt exhilarated. She followed John back up the companionway and was surprised to see the colors of sunset streaking the sky overhead. "We will meet here at sunrise?" she asked.

John nodded. "Do you have something for supper?"

"Yes," Rebecca told him, hoping it was true. If there weren't stores, she knew she would be too tired to go back down to the galley. She watched John walk away, his gait and posture like an old man of forty. Then she turned and hobbled toward her own bed.

Rebecca spent an odd, silent evening, listening to every creak and groan in the ship, imagining that the unguided helm, still tied securely with her father's knots, would somehow sink them yet. But nothing happened. She shared salt pork and hardtack with Major, then slept with him curled up against her side.

John's whooping from the bow woke her the next morning. She sat up, every muscle in her body aching. As she limped into the early sunlight, she whispered a prayer of thanks when she saw three small whaling boats scattered on the calm water. One was still no more than a speck. The other two were closer.

Rebecca hurried to the bulwark and waved, frantic until she saw her mother's overjoyed wave in return. She stood, her hands clasped tightly as the boat got closer. Joseph was sitting beside Mama. Papa stood in the stern, the steering oar in his hands.

"Do you see your friends?" Rebecca called to John, walking toward him.

"I do," he answered. "And Russell is there, lying down. I recognize his shirt."

Rebecca could hear the tone of pure relief in his voice and she said a prayer for Mr. Greene's recovery as she stopped by the bulwark. "Mr. Tildon will have to forgive your father's debt now," she said to John. "You saved his cargo and his ship." He looked so touched that she smiled at him. "And my own life," she added in a quieter voice. "I will be forever grateful, John." An insistent meow at Rebecca's feet startled her, and she laughed aloud, bending to pick up her cat.

"I did nothing alone," John responded after a silence. They exchanged a quick grin, then moved apart, turning to face the oncoming boats again.

Sometimes one day can change a life forever

AMERICAN *Diaries*

Different girls,
living in different periods of America's past
reveal their hearts' secrets in the pages
of their diaries. Each one faces a challenge
that will change her life forever.
Don't miss any of their stories: